Murder in New Orleans

Book 11

A Dodo Dorchester
Mystery

By

Ann Sutton

Solving a murder in the Big Easy is anything but.

After an invitation to visit New Orleans from Miss Lucille Bassett, famous jazz singer, Dodo and company board a luxury ocean liner and head across the pond. The climate, the food and the culture couldn't be more different from England and Dodo considers the whole trip a grand adventure.

Enjoying her role as tourist, Dodo delights in a trip on a steamer down the Mississippi, a visit to an ancient smuggler's dwelling and the hustle and bustle of Bourbon Street. At the top of her wish list, however, is dancing at Miss Bassett's famous jazz club.

On their second day in Louisiana, a terrible murder occurs without any obvious motive. Lucille implores Dodo to take the case as gangsters abound in the Prohibition Era South and have the police department in their pockets.

Dodo agrees but her sleuthing places a loved one in danger and she is torn between solving the crime for her friend or protecting those she loves.

Curl up with this delightful, pager-turner of a whodunnit that will have you on the edge of your seat until the last chapter.

Published by

Wild Poppy Publishing LLC
Highland, UT 84003

Distributed by Wild Poppy Publishing

Cover design by Julie Matern
Cover Design ©2023 Wild Poppy Publishing LLC

Edited by Waypoint Authors

Dedicated to Paul Kersey

Style Note

As an English person who has never lived in the South, writing this book was a challenge. Plus, it is a light-hearted whodunnit, not a treatise on the treatment of Blacks in the South in the 1920s. But this is where Dodo's story took me.

So I hope you will read this book with grace for its limitations.

I am a naturalized American citizen born and raised in the United Kingdom. I have readers in America, the UK, Australia, Canada and beyond. But my book is set in the United Kingdom.

So which version of English should I choose?

I chose American English as it is my biggest audience, my family learns this English and my editor suggested it was the most logical.

This leads to criticism from those in other English-speaking countries, but I have neither the time nor the resources to do a special edition for each country.

I do use British words, phrases and idioms whenever I can (unless my editor does not understand them and then it behooves me to change it so that it is not confusing to my readers).

Titles and courtesy titles of the British nobility are complicated and somewhat dynamic through the ages. Earls, dukes and marquises have titles that are different from their family names. After extensive study on honorary titles and manners of address I have concluded that to the average reader it is all rather confusing and complicated.

Therefore, in an attempt to eliminate this confusion, I have made the editorial decision to call Dodo's father Lord Dorchester rather than Lord Trent and her mother Lady Guinevere rather than Lady Trent.

Cast of Characters

Dorothea 'Dodo' Dorchester - Amateur sleuth, fashion icon
Rupert Danforth - Dodo's boyfriend
Lizzie Perkins - Dodo's lady's maid
Ernest Scott - Rupert's valet

Lucille 'Lulu' Bassett - Famous jazz singer/owner of jazz club
Cy Preston - Lulu's trumpet player
Dex Dolby - Lulu's sax player
Kid - Lulu's club chef and friend
Eula Mae - Lulu's best friend
Clyde - Eula Mae's son

Tucker Dawson - Club owner, admirer of Lulu
Auggie Benoit - Small restaurant owner, romantic admirer of Lulu
Beau Buckley - Admirer of Lulu, successful businessman
Patrick Rigatti - Gangster

Lieutenant Badger - Local police officer
Dr 'Mac' Fossey - Benevolent Society doctor

Table of Contents

Chapter 1

New Orleans, Louisiana, USA
1924

Sizzling, fragrant air, pungent with the aroma of a bouquet of unfamiliar spices, assaulted Lady Dorothea Dorchester's senses as she emerged into the searing Louisiana sunshine. Wide city streets teemed with streetcars and a mélange of humanity of every shade. Sturdy, limestone buildings lined the road, nestled next to clubs and restaurants, as the sound of trumpets and saxophones spilled out, echoing on the breeze. Holding onto her hat, Dodo spun in amazement as cars honked and barreled past, a smile tugging at her lips.

She and her boyfriend, Rupert Danforth, Ernie his valet, and Lizzie her lady's maid, had made the long journey to attend a memorial for a jazz pianist, Lonnie Chapman, who had been killed in London several months before. Dodo had solved the case and Lucille Bassett, a celebrity jazz singer and the dead man's friend, had invited them to a celebration of Lonnie's life.

"Welcome to New Orleans!" announced the cheerful driver with a flourish as Dodo's entourage all stood in similar awe, wondering at the exotic, vibrant world before them.

A stunning, curvy woman shot onto the pavement from a door emblazoned with the word *Lulu's*, to greet them. Lucille Bassett's eyes shone with pride at Dodo's obvious delight.

"Dodo!" she sang in the familiar, lilting contralto that Dodo remembered so well. Trailing clouds of jasmine, she grabbed Dodo's hands and kissed her soundly on both cheeks. "Honey! You made it!" She grabbed Rupert and kissed him on the cheek. "How was the journey, y'all?"

Long, was the first word that came to mind. Leaving Southampton two weeks earlier on the luxury liner the *St. Helena*, they had passed the tip of Florida and swung into the Gulf of Mexico on a tropical storm that sent everyone to their rooms. Though the crossing of the Atlantic had been passable and the food and entertainment first rate, the seasickness had made her more than ready to arrive at the Port of New Orleans.

"Fabulous!" Dodo fibbed. "But I am exceptionally happy to have arrived."

Behind the statuesque Lucille stood a smaller stone building whose arched windows were sheltered from the burning sun by individual, classy, green canopies. Hanging from a metal rod, a swinging sign bore the same elegant script as the door, declaring the club to be *Lulu's*.

"Well, bless your hearts! Now, y'all look like you could do with somethin' to eat," Lucille declared, shooing them all with her arms. "Come on inside."

They all passed through a swanky vestibule and entered a luxurious room that embraced them with moody, purple walls; deep, velvet booths; and bursts of brass. The tang of last night's cigarettes hung in the air.

Dodo pulled at the silk scarf around her neck, for though the windows were open and multiple enormous fans operated at full speed, the air was still hot and muggy.

An expansive, wooden floor for dancing held a raised dais at one end containing an idle drum set and a gleaming, black piano. Small alcoves sheltered by valances and heavy curtains drawn back with decorative tiebacks edged the room.

This was no sleezy *honky tonk,* the kind Dodo had read about in the newspapers. This was a sophisticated establishment that would not have been out of place in London itself.

2

Rupert stuffed his cravat into a pocket while wiping his damp brow with a handkerchief.

Lizzie and Ernie were standing stiff as boards near the entrance.

"Come in!" Lucille encouraged them. "We don't care if you're servants at home. In here, everyone is equal."

Ernie glanced at his fiancée, Lizzie, and shrugged his shoulders before taking her hand and leading her to the counter where Lucille sat on a burnished stool upholstered in blue velvet. The counter faced a bar that was glaringly bare of bottles of spirits.

"Kid!" Lucille cried.

An aging, black man wearing a stain-splotched apron ambled into the room on slightly bowed legs, eyes popping at the sight of the row of white folks sitting at the bar.

"Yes, ma'am?" His gaze never left Lizzie whose cheeks burned scarlet.

"These are the guests I was telling you about, Kid. Now what do you say you bring that delicious food we can smell?"

The chef's face split into the biggest smile revealing a healthy gap between prominent front teeth. He tipped his head with a wink. "Yes, ma'am!"

"I had Kid prepare you some traditional New Orleens' food," explained Lucille. "Gumbo to start followed by jambalaya, with beignets for the sweet."

Dodo's brow creased. Was Lucille speaking another language? "Gumbo?"

Lucille chuckled. "Don't you worry, honey. It's just a thick soup eaten every day in this part of the country. I guarantee ya'll will love it."

Before Lucille had finished speaking, Kid returned, bearing a heavy tray holding four steaming bowls. The mouthwatering odor Dodo had divined outside on the street, now filled the entire room. As Kid leaned over to

3

deliver the gumbo, Dodo noticed a pencil tucked behind his cauliflower ear.

Lizzie tentatively picked up her spoon, taking a miniscule bite. Her face squeezed into a million lines as the unique mixture of flavors walloped her taste buds. She began to cough as Kid doubled over with good-humored laughter, slapping his thigh.

"Woah!" choked Lizzie, tears running down her cheeks.

Undeterred, Dodo dipped in her own spoon, sipping a small amount of the fragrant soup. The combination of spices danced around her mouth, tingling her tongue. However, rather than causing her to choke, her mouth relished the strange, exciting blend. It was like nothing she had ever tasted before.

"Amazing!" she declared. "Hats off to the chef!"

Kid touched his forehead, beaming at her praise.

Beside her, Rupert was tucking in with the energy of a hungry child. "Delicious!"

Ernie had waited, studying everyone's reactions before taking the plunge. His brow smoothed upon seeing his employer eating so heartily. He tried a bite. "Very good, Mr. Kid. Very good indeed!"

The older man grabbed the front of his grubby apron with large, work worn hands. "Maersi, but it's just Kid, sir."

Dodo caught Ernie looking askance at Lizzie. As a valet, he was not used to being called 'sir'. They definitely weren't in England anymore.

Lucille was gauging all their reactions with a hawk eye. "Now, what can I get y'all to drink? No wine, of course, but Kid makes a killer lemonade or iced tea."

Lizzie started in horror.

"Lemonade would be perfect," replied Dodo, noticing that in her own environment, Lucille's accent was far stronger.

4

"Prohibition. I've read about it in the papers, of course, but how does it work in practice?" asked Rupert.

Lucille shook her head slowly. "Kinda hard to run an entertainment business without alcohol, but we manage. Good music and good food. I suppose the bill was passed with the best intentions, but unfortunately, the thorny law has backfired mightily. It's led to the rise of what is being called by the journalists, 'organized crime'."

"What is that?" asked Dodo.

"Gangs of lawless and corrupt men. They produce 'moonshine' whiskey and other spirits and sell it under the table with no regulation and no collection of taxes. It's rough stuff, let me tell you. I wouldn't subject my clientele to that garbage.

"They terrorize businesses like mine, pressuring us to buy their products and extorting money in the name of protecting our business from crime. Ha! From violent gangs like theirs is what that means. They're ruthless and stop at nothing."

"How do they get away with it?" asked Rupert. "Surely the police must try to control them?"

Lucille answered with a mirthless chuckle. "The police? They're all on the take from the mobsters. *And* the judges. They look the other way, lining their pockets with dirty money."

"Is that the reason for the '*speakeasies*'," asked Dodo.

Lucille shrugged. "Yes, ma'am. I think in other cities where the police have resisted the bribes, and the sale of alcohol is truly prohibited, those clubs try to keep their existence a secret so they aren't raided and the owners prosecuted."

Dodo scraped her bowl clean. "And you've never been tempted?"

Lucille quirked a finely plucked brow. "I'd be lying if I said I haven't thought about it, but like I said, we manage and cater to a more upscale crowd. I sell cigars, quality food, cola drinks and provide the best music in town. So far, we're living in high cotton. If that changes, well…" She tipped her head to the side and her full lips tightened. "Can't say I agree with the government forcing this on the population, but I'm darned if I'm gonna let those gangs call the shots."

"Are there many speakeasies in New Orleans?" Dodo patted her tingling lips with a napkin.

Eyes narrowing, Lucille's mouth shrugged. "In downtown they're just about on every corner. They're in the gambling line too. *I* just want to entertain people with good music and world class food."

"I've read about the police raids in Chicago," chimed in Rupert. "But you say that doesn't happen here?"

Smiling, Lucille tapped the counter with painted nails. "Nope. You could drink from a moonshine bottle right outside the police station and they wouldn't bat an eye."

Poor Lizzie was still trying to choke down the gumbo and lunged for the lemonade when it arrived.

Kid whisked the dirty bowls away, whistling a tune, and returned with piping hot plates of something that resembled paella.

"Jambalaya," said Lucille proudly.

Taking a bite, all comparisons with the Spanish dish melted away. Instead of seafood, the spicy rice was filled with tender chicken and an unusual smoked sausage. The seasoning was much milder than in the gumbo.

Anxiety filled Lizzie's face as she scooped up a tiny portion, but relaxed as soon as she tried it.

"Kid! This is wonderful!" declared Dodo.

Pride rolled around his conspicuous features. "Much obliged, Mizz Dorchester!"

"Dorothea is an English Lady, Kid," explained Lucille. "Her father is an earl. You should address her as, 'my lady'."

6

Dodo waved her hands. "Golly no! 'Miss' will work very nicely," she assured the easy-going cook. "I'm well aware that you don't have titles in America."

"If you say so, Mizz Dorchester," said Kid, turning back toward the kitchen.

"How are the preparations for the memorial coming along?" asked Rupert as he shoveled the last remnants of the jambalaya into his mouth.

Lonnie Chapman, Lucille Bassett's friend, mentor, and pianist, had been killed in London a few months before.

Lucille's handsome face lit up. "You're gonna love it! We're gonna have both downtown and uptown bands celebrate his life with a good ol' New Orleen's parade. This city loved that man. It's gonna be an event people won't soon forget." She clapped her hands together. "I declare, it'll be bigger than Mardi Gras!"

Kid returned once more with a silver tray piled high with something golden, covered in white powder that smelled so sweet and comforting that Dodo's mouth watered.

"And now for a treat that will make you want to slap your mama," declared Lucille with a laugh. "Beignets."

Still smiling at the colorful phrase, Dodo reached for one of the honey-colored puffs and bit into the warm, light, fried bread. *Magic!*

"Mmm, mmm," she murmured through white, sugared lips.

This time Lizzie did not hesitate.

Filled to the gills, the English party moved to the comfort of a booth at Lucille's invitation and spent time chatting. However, when Rupert stifled a yawn, Lucille insisted she take them to her home to get settled in and take a nap in preparation for a night at the club. Dodo had assured Lucille that they could stay in a hotel but she wouldn't hear of it.

The driver who had picked them up from the port was still outside leaning against the sleek, black car with its enormous silver grill. Jabbering to a group of young men who scattered, he hurried to open the doors.

Traveling through wide, bustling streets, Dodo thrilled at the multicolored houses with their filigree balconies. A short while later, they pulled off the main street and onto a quiet side road bordered by large oaks draped with some kind of plant that swayed in the breeze like mermaid hair in water.

They stopped in front of a grand, detached house painted entirely white whose front was filled with large windows framed with black shutters. A porch on the ground floor, bordered by a wrought iron railing was matched by one on the upper floor. Inviting rocking chairs and a breakfast table beckoned to weary travelers from the lower porch. In the harsh southern sunlight, the lovely house shone like a pearl.

"This was the home of the famous French painter, Degas," said Lucille as they stood on the pavement. "He died in 1917 and it was bought by a wealthy widow. I walked by it once as a child and would often dream of living here. When *Smokey Syncopation* began to hit it big, I kept my eye on the property. Three years ago, the widow died and I snatched it up. My dream came true!"

"It certainly transcends the ordinary," agreed Dodo as the driver removed their luggage from the back of the car.

Lucille led them up the front steps and onto the porch that offered the perfect spot for relaxation while watching the world go by.

"I have a comfy apartment above the club for convenience, but this is my home," she explained.

Though the entry was narrow, it was bright and full of patterns and texture. An open door on the right revealed a living room that blended elegant design with warmth, and on the left, a tasteful formal dining room. A steep, wooden staircase led to the second floor.

"Degas' mother and grandmother were both born in New Orleens," Lucille explained as she swept down the hall toward the back of the house, past vivid paintings.

"Were they really?" gasped Rupert. "I had no idea."

The old oak floors creaked with a cracked voice revealing a half century of use.

Lucille stopped abruptly and they entered a room of blissful seclusion, full of dreamy appeal and family pictures. The walls, painted an eggshell blue, held pretty sconces. A delicate, marble fireplace anchored one wall, the stage for striking arrangements of tall grasses. On either side of the fire, tall windows stood, like sentinels, framed by beige French drapes. Dodo's mother would have adored it.

"Can I offer you some sweet, iced tea?" Lucille asked before she sat.

"Iced tea?" queried Lizzie.

Ernie was failing to hide his disdain.

"It's too darn hot here for that tea you drink in England. We make it cold and so sweet it'll take the white off your teeth."

"That's very kind of you," said Dodo speaking for everyone. "But I am still full from that magnificent lunch." She rubbed her stomach for emphasis, earning grateful looks from everyone.

"In that case, I'll show you to your rooms. Please follow me."

From a conversation they had when Lucille was in London, Dodo knew that she did not keep a maid or a housekeeper, preferring to pay people to come in and clean weekly.

Surely, she has a cook.

Rather than retracing her steps, Lucille continued on to the back of the house where another staircase was waiting to take them to the upper floor.

The first room, painted a soothing, seafoam green, held a large canopy bed with sheer drapes hanging from its frame.

Lucille turned to Lizzie. "This is your room." Lizzie's jaw dropped before she squealed with delight.

"I think she likes it," said Dodo with a grin.

"You're next door, sugar," she said, addressing Dodo and opening another door. This room was much larger than Lizzie's. Sophisticated, navy walls contrasted with crisp, white trim. It also boasted a canopied bed draped with white sheers but was covered with an eye-catching, dark blue and white counterpane. A tall French window opened onto the balcony.

"Perfect!" declared Dodo.

Instead of plunging onto the enticing, soft bed, Dodo wandered across the hall behind Rupert and Ernest. The valet's room was a good size with the same light blue walls as the drawing room and sturdy oak furniture. Rupert's was a large, square room with a comfortable leather couch at the end of a robust oak bed with four high posts. His room overlooked a pretty garden.

"This will suit me down to the ground," announced Rupert.

Satisfaction shone out of Lucille's comely features. Though Dodo did not know much about the famous singer's past, she knew enough to appreciate that the purchase of this historic house would be considered a great coup.

"Now, if y'all don't mind, I need to get back to the club and get things ready for this evening. I'll send a car to pick you up at nine thirty. That okay?"

"Splendid," replied Dodo. "And it will be just Rupert and I," she whispered. "Lizzie would feel most uncomfortable to be included in the party."

Lucille compressed her lips while raising her brow. "If you say so." She spun on her heels and grabbed the stair railing. "Now, get some rest. Y'all look worn slap out! I'll see you later at the club. Be prepared for a crazy good time!"

Chapter 2

After a refreshing nap, Dodo was excited for the night's entertainment. She was familiar with upscale London jazz clubs, of course, and Rupert's Secret Jazz Parties, or SJPs as they were known, but this evening promised something unconventional.

Knowing that fashions were different in America, Dodo had halted between two opinions as to what to wear to her first visit to Lucille's ritzy jazz club. In the end, she had chosen a black and emerald green, tasseled gown with matching bandeau made with a single ostrich feather. She paired her outfit with long, black gloves and a string of gunmetal gray pearls.

Rupert looked delicious, as always, in an understated suit, his thick, blond hair swept back from his noble brow.

Dodo gazed through the windows of the car with wonder. At night, the crescent city presented a totally different temperament. Flashing lights called from almost every street corner as competing jazz melodies floated into the streets, marrying like frisky snakes. Talented musicians played out on the roads, their brass instruments winking in the streetlights, enticing people to enter. Eager to absorb the magic, she wound down the window, allowing the muggy, warm air and enchanting rhythmic sounds to envelop her senses.

It was unusual for a European's first foray across the pond not to be to New York or New England. But as Dodo breathed in the exhilarating, spicy atmosphere, she doubted Central Park could compete.

When the driver pulled up outside *Lulu's*, a crowd of fashionably dressed people stood in line waiting to enter. She and Rupert joined the end of the queue, attracting more than a sliver of attention. As the familiar sounds of *Smokey*

Syncopation spilled out onto the pavement, Dodo could not resist tapping her toes.

Once inside, thick clouds of smoke curling around the lights caused Dodo to cough. The din of music and chatter was almost deafening. Rupert guided her to the edge of the crowded dance floor. She immediately recognized Cy Preston on the trumpet and Dex Dolby on the saxophone from their visit to England. She waved. They beamed back with their eyes, not missing a note. Curious to see who had replaced Lonnie at the piano, she transferred her gaze to the spindly, young man sliding capable fingers up and down the keys. He wore a smile as big as Sunday on his long, affable face. The three men all wore white trousers and shirts, black jackets and long straight black ties with black, patent leather shoes.

Lucille winked from the stage and smoothed a hand down her figure-hugging, kingfisher gown. Couples swarmed the dance floor as the melody changed and Lucille's velvet tones filled the room with a seductive ballad.

"Care to dance, Lady Dorothea?" asked Rupert, holding up his hand in invitation.

"I'd be honored Mr. Danforth."

Dodo melted into Rupert's strong arms. The familiar scent of his citron cologne embracing her like a hug.

He spoke into her ear, tickling the skin. "Are you refreshed from taking a nap?"

"Goodness, I wouldn't be able to stand up straight if not for a little shut eye. Travel is so terribly tiring."

"I hear you," he agreed. "But it is bally exciting, isn't it? I could never have imagined such a place. Even the air tastes different!"

"I know exactly what you mean!"

The slow song came to an end and the trumpeter hiked up the tempo with one of the band's more popular tunes.

The whole room erupted as people clapped and hollered, hooting in a way unfamiliar to Dodo. It was irresistible.

Dodo's lip curled. "They certainly know how to ramp up the excitement."

"I should say!" agreed Rupert.

The pair of them danced their hearts out until, by the last note, they were quite out of breath and retreated to empty seats in a vacant alcove.

"Please welcome *Kool Katz* to the floor while me and the boys take a break," purred Lucille into the microphone. A group of much younger men took their place on the stage.

Checking the room, Lucille spotted them and made a beeline for their table.

"Can I get you a drink? We have ᶜCoca Cola."

"Cocoa what?" asked Dodo in confusion. She still hadn't adjusted to the notion of cold tea.

"Not cocoa. Coca. ᶜCoca Cola. It's very popular, especially since Prohibition started. It's actually pretty delicious." She raised a hand, signaling to a youthful waiter sporting a wide smile and sparkling, eager eyes. "Three colas, Clyde."

"Yes, ma'am, Mizz Bennett." He hurried away to perform the task.

"Were you able to get any rest?" Lucille asked.

"I had a lovely nap, thank you," replied Dodo pulling up her gloves and adjusting her necklace. "Your bed is very comfortable."

"I'm glad to hear it." Lucille flicked some hair from her face. She had admitted to Dodo that she wore wigs every day. This one was long, silky, and straight. "What about you, Rupert?" she asked.

"I actually went for a stroll around your lovely neighborhood. Love the architecture. So different from home."

14

"I'm glad you like it," she responded as the cheerful waiter returned with a circular tray containing three unusual bottles. The glass was twisted at the top and a tall, candy-striped stick poked from the top. He handed one to each of them. Lucille took hers and put her lips to the tall stick. Bemused, Dodo and Rupert watched with interest.

She flicked the red and white item. "It's a straw. Try it!"

Dodo picked up the cool, sweating bottle, placed the straw in her mouth and sucked hard. Before she knew it, a mass of bubbles shot into her mouth and up her nose.

"Ack!" She threw her head back and slammed the bottle to the table, grabbing the bridge of her nose. "Ouch!"

Lucille and the pleasant waiter curled up with laughter.

"Boy, howdy! I get such a kick out of first-timers," the waiter chuckled. "The first time I tried it, thought I was drownin'."

Rupert, who had not yet taken a sip, bent toward Dodo with concern. She flapped her hands as the sensation ebbed away. "You could have warned me, Lucille!"

"Ah, but that would have been a lot less fun. And it's Lulu." The singer wiped her eyes. "Try again but take a little sip this time."

Someone beckoned to the waiter she had called Clyde.

"It's fizzy," Dodo warned Rupert. "That's all."

She took a smaller swig, allowing the pleasant, sugary taste to sit in her mouth before swallowing. "Mmm. That *is* good."

Lucille pushed the straw around with her finger. "That drink has saved my business, really. It's considered an acceptable replacement for the hard stuff."

Rupert took a drink. "Mmm. It's really good. What's it called again?"

"Coca Cola."

A middle-aged woman whom Dodo's grandmother would have described as mutton dressed as lamb, slipped onto a chair in their alcove and placed a proprietary arm

15

around Rupert. She looked Dodo up and down as if the wind was blowing upwind from a pig farm.

Dodo bristled.

"Eula Mae," said Lucille in a warning tone. "Be nice to my guests."

"I am," declared the woman using two syllables to pronounce each word in a voice that sounded like she ate razor blades for breakfast. She withdrew her arm and beamed, revealing a crowded row of oversized, yellow teeth.

"This is my best friend, Eula Mae," said Lucille by way of introduction. "She can misbehave at times."

Eula Mae threw back a head of smooth curls and cackled like a witch. "Me misbehave? Why I'm as pure as a priest on Sunday." Her accent was a great deal stronger than Lucille's. She held out a hand that had seen plenty of hard work and shook, first with Dodo. "Ain't you pretty as a peach!" Then more firmly with Rupert, not letting go. "Y'all didn't fall out 'a no ugly tree, sugar."

Rupert was clearly amused by the whole situation.

Dodo rolled her eyes.

"Put him down, Eula Mae," warned Lucille. "I told you, he's spoken for."

Lucille's friend growled like a lioness. "If y'all insist. But you didn't tell me how pretty he was." She turned her face to Rupert, still gripping his hand. "You'd win first prize at the county fair, ain't no mistakin'."

Dodo swallowed a grin.

"Eula Mae and I have been friends since we were kids. She runs the bar and food for me."

The over-friendly woman raised a dark brow. "I do." Pushing a shoulder forward while pursing her lips, she explained. "Lucille and her daddy came through for me when my mama died. We lived downtown then." The flirtation receded like a wave on a beach and a different woman sat before them. "I owe Lulu everything."

16

"Well, other than the fact that you can start an argument in an empty house, you do a good job. Else I might fire you and find someone else." Lucille chuckled, diffusing the serious mood.

"You won't never fire me," declared Eula Mae, returning to the playful tone and slapping Rupert's knee. "You'd never find no one else who could put up with ya." The cackling began again in earnest as she stood.

"Now, what can I get for y'all? Curds? Chitlins? Boudin? Grits?"

Dodo's head was spinning.

Lucille smacked her friend on the arm. "Will you stop teasing these poor folk, Eula Mae?" She turned herself to face Dodo and Rupert. "Those items are for the locals, but we also have a proper menu."

Sultry eyes fixed firmly on Rupert, Eula Mae continued. "We serve crawdads and oysters, Louisiana style a' course. Gumbo and muffaletta."

"Muffaletta is an Italian sandwich with ham, salami, and olive oil in the best bread you ever tasted," explained Lucille. "It's one of my personal favorites."

"Then I shall try that," said Rupert.

"I'll have the crawdads," said Dodo, though Eula Mae was barely aware of her presence.

"Comin' right up!" She threaded through the crowd on thin legs and high heels.

Lucille shook her head slowly. "You gotta love her though she can make me madder 'an a wet hen at times. We both grew up downtown, for the most part, but she can't shed that part of herself. I hope she didn't cause offense?"

"Not at all," Dodo assured her, still a little stunned by the flamboyant woman.

"Cher, Lulu." An average man in every way was leaning against the alcove wall, smoking a cigar. Dodo tried to hold her breath.

17

"Hello, Auggie." There was little enthusiasm in Lucille's tone.

He held the cigar tight between crooked front teeth. "You considered my offer?"

Lucille's eyelids closed slowly as she took a deep, slow breath. "I told you, Auggie, I'm not ready to marry yet. I'm enjoying life just fine, thank you. Quit wasting your time."

A proposal?

Dodo examined the man more closely. He wore his hair extremely short and a trim mustache gave relief to an otherwise plain face.

"I'm a patient man, Lulu. I'll be here when you're ready. *A plus tard.*" He lifted a stubby chin and sauntered off, soon swallowed by the large crowd.

Dodo cocked an eyebrow at Lucille.

"I would *never* marry that man," Lucille rushed to explain. "He's… not my type. But he's persistent, I'll give him that."

The waiter stopped by their table with a steaming tray of crawdads and the Italian sandwich.

"Clyde! Stop a minute. Come and meet my new friends properly." She placed a hand on his arm. "This here is Eula Mae's son. He's a fine boy. Her pride and joy."

An infectious smile began to sprout which finally took over Clyde's whole face.

"It's a pleasure to meet you," said Dodo, catching his eye.

"How do you do?" Rupert offered a hand. The boy looked at the tray and back at Rupert as if confused.

"Put the tray down and shake the man's hand," suggested Lucille.

His long arm leaned down and the tray of food slid onto the table. Tentatively, he took Rupert's hand, staring as their skin touched.

"Clyde!" The harsh voice of his mother fractured the smooth sound of the jazz.

18

His whole face shrugged. "I'd better scram." He bowed to Dodo and ran off on spindly legs.

"He's a good boy," began Lucille. "He was conceived in less than ideal circumstances that left his mother afraid and alone – except for Daddy and me. And the birth was long and difficult and caused some…problems. But he's a fine worker and trustworthy which is more than I can say for some folks." She pointed to the food. "Don't let it get cold."

Dodo's hand hesitated over the large, red shellfish that resembled an enormous prawn or small lobster.

"Just grab the tail and the head and twist," explained Lucille. "Then pull the tail from the head and peel the shell off the tail. Simple."

Dodo broke open the first shell and placed the soft, white meat into her mouth. "Wow! So sweet!"

Rupert took a huge bite of the sandwich, eyes popping out of his head. "I've never tasted anything like it," he explained once he had swallowed. "The bread is out of this world."

"The bread recipes are from the French who owned the land before the Louisiana Purchase. Best in the world, I say. Though I must admit, your English bread was pretty good too."

"The Louisiana Purchase? Wasn't that when the French sold the area to the United States for a pittance in the last century?" asked Rupert.

"Sure is. That's why we have folks who speak Creole. It's a mix of French and various African dialects and you must have noticed all the French street names during your stroll."

A shadow was cast over their table. "Gonna introduce me to your fancy friends, Lulu?" The big man would not have looked out of place at a Scottish pole tossing contest.

"Tucker Dawson," responded Lucille with a small smile, pulling her green boa up her arm. "Tucker here is one of the other club owners in this district. He wants to buy '*Lulu's*', but it ain't for sale." Her tone was almost lazy.

Tucker rubbed his pocked cheeks. "You could retire on what I give you and concentrate all your energies on your sensational singing."

"I manage just fine, thanks," replied Lulu. "As I've told you countless times."

He tugged on his expensive jacket lapels. "Can't blame a man for trying." He tipped his square head to Dodo and Rupert. "And who might these fine folks be?"

"These here are my friends from England. Mizz Dorchester, solved the murder of Lonnie. They've come as my guests for the memorial."

"This pretty, little lady is a detective?" His voice was as scarred as his skin. He grabbed a chair, turned it around and sat, with forearms like hams, leaning on the back of it. "I thought the English were all about tea and the king."

Dodo chuckled and leaned into his charisma. "I hope there's a little more to us than that."

Tucker pulled out a cigarette case but as Lucille frowned, he thought better of it and snapped the case shut, sliding it back into his breast pocket. "I'm just an ign'ant American. Don't mind me. I'm just surprised, is all."

"It *is* unusual," Dodo admitted. "But I'm pretty good at sleuthing and I like to think I make the world a little better with each case I solve."

"You can solve a case for me any day, darlin'."

"Tucker, Mr. Danforth here and Mizz Dorchester are a couple," warned Lucille.

Tucker snapped his head to Rupert, beefy hand extended. "Apologies. No harm done. You're a lucky man."

"I know," replied Rupert, clearly amused as the man pumped his hand.

Lucille looked at her watch. "Time for me to get back on stage. Perhaps you can play the host for my friends, Tucker?"

"I'd be honored, ma'am." In spite of his rougher appearance, he seemed like a perfect gentleman. A stark contrast to Auggie, the persistent proposer.

As they watched Lucille slink away, Tucker let out a whistle. "That woman is somethin', ain't she?"

Dodo examined his face as he kept his eyes on Lucille, making it obvious he was interested in more than just her business.

"She is very capable," agreed Rupert.

Tucker shifted his chair closer to the table and lowered his voice. "Capable but still needs protectin'. It's a cutthroat business."

"Protection?" asked Dodo.

He pulled his lips so far up, his cheeks swelled, and his eyes squinted but it couldn't be described as a smile. "I guess you folks don't know about the gangster problem, bein' foreigners."

"Lulu mentioned they had become a constant problem since Prohibition," said Dodo.

"Then allow me to give you a little history lesson. Prohibition, the government forcing people not to drink, is passed by Congress in 1920. Ya think that's gonna work? 'Course not. So, what happens? People start makin' their own. But the criminally minded see this as a great opportunity to make bucket loads of money and control the illegal distribution of the booze through violence." He flicked a hand toward their cola bottles. "That stuff is only as good as it goes. People crave their alcohol, right? It's addictive. So, a gangster by the name of Ricci begins his reign of terror. Controls the town and the police department who're all on his payroll. But one of Ricci's mobsters wants the top job and knocks him off. Fella by the name of Rigatti. He's worse than his old boss."

21

"How exactly does that affect Lucille?" asked Dodo.

"The gangsters don't like places like this that keep the law and serve only soda. They see it as lost revenue and try to shake 'em down. Extort 'em for money to 'protect' their interests."

"Is that how the speakeasies get their liquor?" asked Rupert.

"Exactly!" replied Tucker. "Now you're gettin' the picture."

"Have they tried to pressure Lucille?" asked Dodo.

"Course they have. But she turns 'em down. She's a brave woman. They leave her alone for a while then ramp up their persuasion tactics. That's why I want to buy this place. Protect Lulu from dangerous criminals."

A real Good Samaritan.

Chapter 3

"Now, if you'll excuse me," said Tucker. "I have some business to attend to."

Watching the wolf in sheep's clothing stalk away, Dodo growled. "I've changed my mind. I don't like him at all."

"Me neither," agreed Rupert.

As Tucker disappeared into the throng, Dodo remembered her unfinished meal. Polishing off the last of the shellfish, she licked her fingers—something she would never do at home.

"I take it you enjoyed those," said Rupert with a smile. "My sandwich was delicious too. And this cola stuff is great once you get used to it."

Dodo wiped her hands with a napkin. "I thought I was quite well rounded in the exotic food department but this is a blend of herbs and spices I never imagined existed."

Rupert tilted his head in the direction Tucker had left. "Why don't you like him?"

Dodo wiggled her shoulders. "Something about him…makes my stomach turn. All that poppycock about wanting to buy the place to *save* Lucille."

Rupert grinned. "Same here. He certainly oozes charm but it disguises the snake beneath."

Satisfactorily full, both Rupert and Dodo leaned back in their seats to savor the soulful music of *Smokey Syncopation*. Dodo's eyes drifted to the replacement pianist. There was no doubt he had masterful control of the keys, but he was just shy of the quality of his predecessor, Lonnie. As her eyes wandered further around the room, she saw a couple of posters announcing the grand memorial for Lonnie Chapman, in just a week's time.

Lucille's chic club was bursting at the seams and she was undoubtedly earning a tidy income, on top of her earnings from the band. *Lulu's* was open every night of the week—even Sundays. She clearly had no need of advice from the likes of Tucker Dawson.

The tempo picked up and Rupert stood. "Ready to burn off some of that food, darling?"

Dodo took his hand as they eased onto the busy dance floor amid more inquisitive stares.

Before coming to New Orleans, Dodo had thought her own set danced well but witnessing the energetic and spirited styles at *Lulu's*, she readjusted her thinking and tried to copy their unique gyrations.

Even with the large fans overhead, the room was unbearably warm and Dodo was sticky with sweat after just one lively dance. They wandered to the back of the club seeking fresh air outside.

As they squeezed past people surrounding the door, Dodo was delightfully surprised to find an attractive patio area. Rectangular tables provided seating al fresco for at least thirty people and potted trees lined the edges. Strings of lights hung between the trees creating a romantic ambiance. And a gentle, albeit warm breeze, gave relief from the stuffiness of the club.

A tall, solid fellow was talking to Kid, at what Dodo realized was the kitchen door—a separate, smaller building at the bottom of the patio area. Kid indicated them to the man, who turned around and stared with blatant interest. He was an extremely handsome man in his early forties.

With a broad smile that matched his step and animated dark eyes, he hustled over and pulled out a chair.

Jabbing the air, he spoke with a friendly voice that reminded Dodo of the smooth tones of a double bass. "Howdy! You must be those highfalutin' folks from England. The ones that helped Lucille find out who killed poor Lonnie."

How come Lucille had never mentioned this captivating gentleman who clearly had intimate knowledge of the inner workings of Lucille's life?

"Spot on!" responded Rupert. "I'm Rupert Danforth and this is my girlfriend, Dorothea Dorchester. It's a pleasure to meet you Mr. …?" His eyes held a question.

"Didn't I…?" The amiable man slapped his forehead. "No, I guess I didn't. Sometimes I'm useless as gum on a boot heel." He wiggled his fingers. "Name's Beau Buckley." Putting both arms at right angles, he made the motion of a steam engine's wheels, leaving one hand up high for Rupert to shake. Dodo felt an immediate bond with this teddy bear of a fellow who overflowed with contagious energy.

White teeth caught the dim light as a smile split his attractive face. "And you, Mizz Dorothea, are cute as a bug's ear."

Returning the infectious smile she responded, "I'm not sure what that means but I'll take it as a compliment. Thank you."

"It sure is!" He rubbed his big hands together.

"I'm sure Lucille told you all about me while she was in London." Pulling his lips in, his dark eyes rolled from side to side.

He should be on the stage!

"Well—"

Lucille hadn't mentioned this man once, but Dodo was saved from embarrassment by the arrival of the singer herself.

"Beau Buckley! Are you behaving yo'self?" Lucille seemed to slip on a new persona in Beau's presence.

Beau beamed. "Of course, honey!"

"Don't you 'honey' me," she declared, slapping his arm. But the expression on her face told a different story. "This low life giving you trouble?" she asked Dodo.

25

Dodo held up both palms. "Not in the least. We were just being introduced."

Lucille's brow made a show of darkening. "Did he spin some yarn about him being my sweetheart?"

Beau's chin dipped as his eyes bugged.

"He did, didn't he? How many times do I have to tell you, Beau, we are not a couple?" Hands on hips, Lucille pretended to glower but there was more chemistry in the air than with either of the other two swains. She might profess disinterest but she was lying to herself. "He asks me to marry him every Saturday. It's more annoying than a box of mosquitos at a church picnic!"

This flirty side of Lucille had not emerged in London.

Beau reached for her hand, but she ignored him. "One 'a these days she's gonna say, yes!"

Lips pinched tight as if she'd sucked on a lemon, Lucille declared, "You see! Loopy as a cross-eyed cowboy." She banged on the tabletop. "Kid! Bring me some gumbo!"

"Comin' right up, Mizz Lulu," Kid cried from the door to the kitchen.

In a softer tone, Lucille protested, "I'm parched. Go fetch me a cola, Beau."

Eager as a puppy, the big man jumped to his feet and scurried inside.

Treading carefully, Dodo said, "He seems rather nice."

"Oh, he's nice enough," said Lucille, fanning herself. "I've known him for years, now. Always trying to give me advice on how to run this place. I'm doing just fine by myself. Why do all these men think I'm helpless?"

Lucille's father and his pianist had started the club together some years before. Then her father had deeded his portion to her before his death. Now that Lonnie had died and left his half of the business to Lucille in his will, she was the sole proprietor. Dodo imagined that running this type of business presented a challenge for a woman, with plenty of vultures circling. It might not be a bad thing to have someone like Beau in her corner.

"Does he really propose every Saturday?" Dodo asked.

The hard lines on Lucille's face softened. "Every week, like clockwork. He's more persistent than Auggie."

"But don't you want to marry?" asked Dodo with genuine interest. She put Lucille's age at about thirty-five.

"I'm too busy clawing my way up in my career. No time for men." She quieted and tapped her fingers on the top of the table. "It's not that I'm opposed to the institution and if someone came and swept me off my feet, I might change my mind." She tipped her head toward Rupert who was busy watching Kid approach. "Like your sugar pie."

It was true that Dodo's was a match of true love, but she still did not have a ring and sometimes wondered what Rupert was waiting for. Was it to finish his London townhome? Was he waiting for a special date like Christmas? She had no doubts that he felt the same way about her, and he had hinted at marriage on more than one occasion. So, what was he waiting for?

"I'm very lucky," Dodo agreed, drinking in the familiar, beloved lines of Rupert's profile.

"One mighty fine bowl of gumbo, Mizz Bassett," croaked Kid, slapping the bowl on the table. "Allons manger!"

"Mmmm, mmm," Lucille declared as the scent of the soup rose like the flickering flames of a fire. "All that singing makes a girl hungry."

Beau returned with the bottle of cola and placed it on the table in front of Lucille.

"Thank you, Beau."

His whimsical expression indicated that he was grateful for any little crumb of appreciation.

After the usual small talk Rupert asked, "How did you find your new pianist? He has amazing talent."

Lucille stirred the gumbo with her spoon. "News of Lonnie's death spread pretty quick, and people just showed up on my doorstep asking to audition. Before I was ready, really. But after a bit, I realized that the best way to honor Lonnie was to keep performing. So, I started holding proper auditions. That boy was number seventeen. I knew I'd found a replacement the minute his fingers hit the keys." She took a sip of the cola. "No one will ever play quite like Lonnie, but he's a pretty good substitute."

"Come on! That boy's amazin' and gettin' better 'n better," chimed in Beau.

"If I want your opinion, Beau Buckley, I will ask for it!" Lucille snapped but with no real zing in her tone. Rather than take offense, the larger-than-life Beau, melted into a puddle at her feet.

A sudden scuffle at the back door to the club captured their attention. Lucille groaned. Beau stiffened gripping the edge of the table. A short, stocky, white man wearing a hat and dark suit pushed his way onto the patio. Even in the dusky light, Dodo could see that one of the man's eyes was clouded with small scars around the socket. His good eye roved around the tables, stopping on Dodo, undressing her with his eye.

She shuddered.

"Patrick Rigatti. What are *you* doin' here? I don't remember sendin' you an invite," hissed Lucille.

"You know me, Lulu. Open invitation to visit any establishment on my turf." He was still gawking at Dodo as he spoke. Determined not to show fear, she held his gaze defiantly, though he definitely made her skin crawl. Rupert slid a protective arm around the back of her chair and Dodo could sense the tension rolling off him.

Lucille's eyes narrowed. "Who died and made you the king? Oh, wait! You! You killed Ralphie Ricci and crowned yourself."

He checked his cuffs, showing off short, fat fingers full of gaudy rings. "Be careful what you say, Mizz Bassett, or I might have to take you to court for slanderin' my good name."

"Hmphh! Good name? I think you lost that a long time ago," spat Lucille.

Mr. Rigatti took a step forward and both Rupert and Beau jumped up. Rigatti moved the front of his coat aside to reveal a gun tucked into the waistband of his pants. Neither man moved. Dodo's heart caught in her throat.

"You can't hold out for long," sneered Rigatti. "All your neighbors have…joined the fold. You'll soon be losing customers."

"Folks come to *Lulu's* because we have the best music in town," she snapped back.

"Can't disagree there," he said, "but think how much money we would make in partnership." He leered at Dodo again. "But I can see you have some classy company." He touched his hat. "I'll be back, Lulu."

As the disgusting man left, Lucille growled. "That man makes me crankier than a drunk racoon in a corn maze. He thinks the sun comes up just to hear him crow! If I thought it would do any good, I'd call the police and report him for harassment."

"Why wouldn't it?" asked Rupert.

"That there man is our local gangster," explained Beau. "He bribes the police chief. Has the whole department in his pocket. Not to mention every judge in town too. Crooked, the whole lot of 'em!"

"Is he an extortionist?" asked Dodo.

Lulu pouted. "He's way more than that, darlin'. Controls the entire neighborhood."

"I don't understand. Why don't you all just challenge him?" asked Dodo.

"Because he settles disputes with a Tommy gun. Kills anyone who opposes him," began Lucille. "See, the passing of Prohibition created a hole. People still want alcohol no matter what the government tries to force on folks. For the likes of Pat Rigatti, this becomes an opportunity to give the people what they want *and* take control of the market. The gangsters, headed by Rigatti, make the illegal spirits and eliminate the competition. Then they strong-arm businesses like mine to buy the booze from them to sell illegally. Complete shakedown at the end of a barrel.

"Rigatti was number three in the organization not six months ago but number one was responsible for blinding him in that one eye last year and he was boiling with revenge. He had numbers one and two killed off and made himself the head of the family, as they call it." She took a deep, shaky breath. "Most of my neighbors have surrendered. But I'm darned if I'm going to let little Patty Rigatti from the old neighborhood push *me* around. My business is clean and I want it to stay that way."

"He threatens Lucille almost as much as I propose to her," said Beau, the good humor drained completely out of his voice. "I wish…" He punched the palm of his sizeable hand.

Chapter 4

Though the visit of Patrick Rigatti had been a major black eye on a wonderful evening, the rest of the night passed without incident. This morning, Dodo and Rupert were enjoying a late breakfast on the idyllic porch of Lucille's house, immersed in early morning Louisiana sunshine. Still mesmerized by the magnetic dance of the long strands of moss that gave the wide street its romantic feel, Dodo dug into the pile of fresh pastries. They were almost as good as the ones she ate in Paris.

Lucille arrived halfway through, wearing a gorgeous silk kimono and lilac turban.

"How are you enjoying our New Orleens weather? Nothing but clouds and rain in London. Makes a nice change, don't it?"

"There's no denying you have lovely climate," agreed Dodo, sunbeams warming her face as she ate. "And these pastries are delicious."

Lucille plonked herself down and poured rich, black coffee from a silver pot. She drank the coffee strong and black. *Bitter.*

"Best food in these United States, in my opinion," Lucille said after a calming sip.

"I've been trying to figure out what the spice blend is and I can't quite put my finger on it," commented Dodo.

"It's called Cajun. It's a mash-up of West African, French, Spanish, and American Indian. Nothing like it in the whole world."

Rupert chuckled. "Wow! That *is* a unique blend."

Lizzie and Ernest came out onto the porch and Lucille gestured for them to sit at the table. Lizzie checked that this was acceptable to her mistress. Dodo smiled. Ernest looked most uncomfortable and sat on the chair's edge without touching the back.

"Are you finding everything you need?" Lucille asked them.

"Mostly, but I can't find an iron and the cook says you don't have one, but that can't be right?" replied Lizzie. Dodo had been relieved to learn that the famous singer *did* keep a cook.

Lucille clapped her hands together. "She's right, honey! I send all my washing to the cleaners. *They* do the ironing."

A splash of color dotted Lizzie's cheeks. "Oh."

"I can tell you the address if you need something pressed," said Lucille as the cook, Bernice, brought out an amber color liquid in a glass pitcher and poured a tall glass for Lucille.

"*I* might need it for Mr. Danforth's shirts," said Ernie.

"Why didn't you come to the club last night, sugar?" Lucille asked Lizzie. "You know you're welcome."

"I wanted to get Lady Dorothea's clothes ready for today and then I felt like an early night," Lizzie assured her.

Lucille reached out to grab one of the jammy delicacies but stopped midway. "But you'll come to the memorial?"

"Certainly," said Lizzie. Ernie nodded in agreement.

Dodo glanced at her maid. She knew Lizzie was struggling with the culture; the spiciness of the food, the tea being different. Add to that the closeness of the humid heat and Lizzie was feeling quite homesick.

Dodo thought back to the moment she had offered Lizzie the chance to travel to America. She had squealed, eyes shining like a child's before a birthday party. But the length of the journey, the unfamiliar food and drinks had put a dent in the adventure and Dodo worried that Lizzie was regretting her choice.

Dodo offered her a pastry. "It's just like in France."

Lizzie took a tentative bite before her whole face relaxed. Here was something that tasted like home. Dodo saw her nod to Ernie who reached for his own pastry.

32

"Miss Bassett," Ernie ventured, after swallowing a mouthful. "I'm rather interested in the history of the city. It's unlike any place I've ever been."

Placing her elbows on the arm rests of her chair she replied, "Well, I'm no historian and I didn't pay enough attention in school, but the gist is, that the French settled the area followed by the Spanish and then it went back to the French. Then the United States government bought it for a song in a deal called the Louisiana Purchase. My ancestors were brought here as slaves to work the cotton fields. You see, the climate here is perfect for it. But if you want to know more, I can send you to a friend of mine whose nickname is the *professor*. They know all about the history."

"I would very much like to meet him," said Ernie enthusiastically.

"It's a 'she'," said Lucille with a sly grin.

"I stand corrected," said Ernie, pinching his lips.

The kimono slipped off one shoulder, revealing a mother of pearl, silk negligée. Ernie averted his eyes.

"I'll give her a call, sugar."

"How can we help with the arrangements for the memorial?" asked Dodo.

Lucille raised a hand. "Everythin' is under control. Don't you worry your pretty little head about it. You're here as my guests, and I wanna show you 'round. I'm proud of my hometown. Thought we'd start by takin' a paddleboat steamer out on the Mississippi today."

She poured some of the amber liquid into Dodo and Rupert's glasses. Dodo picked it up and took a gulp, immediately regretting it. Ice-cold tea! It was so sickly sweet you could stick a spoon straight up in it. She tried not to shudder and placed the glass back on the table. Seeing that Rupert was about to pick up his, she sent a warning glare and he thought better of it.

33

"Plus, there's the white cathedral at Jackson square and the old *Lafitte* blacksmith place—"

Lucille was suddenly interrupted by the speedy arrival of Beau, who skated up to the porch like a baseball player sliding into base, hand clamped to his hat.

"Why, Beau Buckley! What are you doing showing up here disturbin' my breakfast like a cross-eyed mule?"

"I take it you haven't read the paper, Lucille?" His chest was rising and falling as fast as he had arrived.

She flicked her manicured fingers toward him. "You know I don't read the paper until at least noon, Beau. What's got you so riled up?"

His face paled. "The *Hurdy Gurdy Club* on Franklin? Got blown up last night."

Lucille slammed the table with both hands. "Is this some kind of a joke, Beau? 'Cause it ain't funny."

"No, ma'am. At around five this mornin' the whole place blew to smithereens."

Lucille's smooth complexion acquired a haggard mien as her hands covered her mouth. "Rigatti?"

"The papers ain't saying, Lulu. But you know as well as I do, the *Hurdy Gurdy* wouldn't agree to his demands."

Dodo checked Lucille as the singer's eyes shone. She allowed Beau to take her hand.

"Was anyone hurt?" she whispered.

"Nah. The place had closed up for the night. But anyone could have been there, the cleaners, the stockmen. Don't bear thinkin' about."

Lucille stifled a sob. "This darned Prohibition! Hands over power to the likes of Rigatti. That man has no conscience."

"Won't the police investigate at all?" asked Rupert.

"Oh, they'll make a show of investigatin' to placate the Feds, but like we told you, they're all on the take. They'll conclude that it was *persons unknown*."

"Has this happened before?" asked Dodo.

34

"'Bout every six months there's a fire or somethin' but never an explosion," said Beau, reaching out to hold Lucille's hand in both of his. She didn't snatch it away. "I think it's time you got some security, Lucille. You don't want all your hard work eliminated in one big boom."

As Lucille's shoulders shook, Beau placed an arm around her. She shrugged him off, wiped her tears, and made to stand. "Please excuse me. I must go and see Frankie. Offer my condolences."

"Want me to come?" asked Beau.

She closed wet eyes and nodded. "I'd like that."

Lucille left to change, leaving the group of visitors agog on the porch.

"Surely the police must do *something*. Or the city councilmen," murmured Rupert.

"There's things you out-of-towners just don't 'preciate," replied Beau. "Rigatti has this city by the throat. The whole city council was elected by the strong-arm tactics of Rigatti's gangsters. The mayor is merely his puppet. It's Rigatti who runs this town."

"And you believe it's because of Prohibition?" asked Dodo.

"No question," replied Beau. "No legislation gonna stop folks wantin' their beer and spirits. So, it opens up a black market. Now the head of that market is in charge—Rigatti. You saw how he was with Lucille last night. She's one of the last holdouts along with the *Hurdy Gurdy*. That bombin' is a warning to her—join me or suffer the consequences."

"I thought the Wild West was a thing of the past," said Dodo.

Beau sighed. "It's alive and well, and Rigatti is the sheriff."

Chapter 5

Though visibly rattled after her return from a visit to the owner of the *Hurdy Gurdy Club* downtown, Lucille had insisted they continue with their afternoon plans on the Mississippi River.

The steamboat was a white beauty with two large steam towers at one end, a magnificent paddle wheel at the other and three passenger decks. Multiple flags were posted on huge poles, snapping in the breeze.

Dodo and Rupert were currently on the top deck with Lucille and Beau while Lizzie and Ernie had wandered off on their own. Dodo decided not to mention the bombing unless Lucille brought it up, but the strain on her face and the trembling of her hands showed that she was horribly shaken by the devastation.

As a daily pleasure cruiser, the ship had no cabins. Instead, each deck of the steamboat contained spacious dining and dancing rooms. As they sailed along the river, passing the white St. Louis Cathedral, the agreeable sound of a small jazz band reached them from the far end of the boat. The river was smooth and the refreshing wind was a welcome relief from the constant, cloying humidity. Dodo hung back her head, eyes closed.

"Hungry for some lunch?" asked Beau with an arm around the uncharacteristically docile Lucille.

"I'm still full from breakfast," said Rupert.

"Me too," agreed Dodo. "Perhaps later."

"Then if you don't mind, Lucille and I are going for a cola."

"No problem. We'll stroll around the deck," assured Dodo.

"I don't know about you, but I feel like a bit of an interloper, given the circumstances," admitted Dodo, leaning on the railing after Lucille and Beau strolled away. "The bombing has changed everything."

"I know what you mean," said Rupert, a gust of wind playing with his wavy hair. "But we can hardly leave before the memorial."

"Agreed, but I want to shrink until I am almost invisible so as not to take up any of Lucille's energy. And on top of losing Lonnie. It's too awful!"

"This town hides an ugly underbelly. I've read in the English papers about a similar situation in Chicago," said Rupert. "The gangsters kill indiscriminately, thumbing their noses at the authorities, wielding fear to subject ordinary people to their demands. It really is a shocking state of affairs."

"It's simply criminal that the police have no power over them, excuse the pun. Utter lawlessness," she responded, warmly.

"Perhaps the best solution is to assure Lucille that we can make our own entertainment over the next few days and plan to leave immediately after the memorial," he suggested.

A pleasant rush of air ruffled her organza frock. "I'd say that was a good plan, darling."

Rupert took her hand and they ambled around the top deck, enjoying the sights beyond the river banks and the young families on board.

"What do you think about children?" she asked as they passed two young girls waving madly at those along the shore.

"I was one not so long ago," he chuckled.

She tipped her parasol and bounced it on the top of his head. "Hardy, ha ha!"

"The idea of being a father is both thrilling and terrifying, but I imagine it's been that way since Adam and Eve."

Dodo considered his answer. "Would you like a whole passel or just one or two?"

Rupert kept his gaze on the riverbanks. "Depends on whether I'm trying for a polo or a cricket team, I suppose."

Dodo descended into a fit of giggles.

He turned to face her. "But seriously, I think it's something best to decide as you go along."

As usual, it was the perfect answer.

"Fancy a cola?" he asked, as they finished the loop.

"Do you know, I'm getting to quite like it," she responded.

Lizzie and Ernest had declined a second invitation to attend the club, saying they had experienced enough excitement for one day. Dodo concluded that Lizzie might consider *Lulu's* to be a den of iniquity that would taint her by association, and let them be. Her own excitement for the evening was at an all-time low due to the terrible news from that morning, but she wanted to support Lucille through the difficult time and caving to the bullies was not the way.

"Ready?" asked Rupert. "There's a car waiting outside." Standing at her door in a remarkably casual, light gray suit, an arm bracing the door jamb, Dodo felt her heart squeeze.

"You look amazing, as usual," he whispered in her ear sending a satisfying shiver down her spine. As his warm hand made contact with her bare shoulder, her skin leapt in response.

The club was only a mile from Lucille's home. She had left earlier than usual to take an active role in the preparations. Dodo suspected that she needed to keep her mind off the bombing and its ramifications. Plus, Lucille could be worried her staff would not show up for work out of fear. Which was a legitimate concern. As soon as they had returned from the pleasure cruise, Lucille had left with Beau to hire a security team.

Now, as Dodo and Rupert entered the club, they saw muscular men in dark suits placed strategically around the room. Even tonight's music carried a somber tone, and rather than dancing, the patrons were all sitting in small groups at tables, huddled in low conversations. The explosion had achieved its purpose and shaken the whole town to its core. The patrons were much less interested in Dodo and Rupert's presence than they had been the night before.

Once settled, Eula Mae wandered over and Dodo braced. Tonight, Eula Mae was dressed in a conservative, black frock and the coquettish persona was nowhere in sight.

"Can you believe it?" she asked. "I've known the owner of the *Hurdy Gurdy* since I was little. He's as lost as last year's Easter egg, poor soul. His life's work, gone in a flash! And rumor is he didn't have no insurance." She made a fist. "I could knock Rigatti into the middle of next week!"

"It is ghastly," agreed Dodo. "But I think Lucille is wise to beef up her security."

"Lotta good it'll do if they're on Rigatti's payroll." Eula Mae tsked. "Now, what can I get for you folks, tonight?"

"I'll take gumbo, please," replied Dodo.

"Same for me," said Rupert.

Dodo looked around the room for any familiar faces. She saw Tucker Dawson sitting in a corner smoking a cigar and tucking into a steaming dish and Auggie just coming through the door, his eyes scanning for Lucille. She glanced at the clock. It was just on ten. Lucille and Beau were out of sight. They must be in the yard out back.

The current band had a different sound to *Smokey Syncopation*, rougher, more twangy. Dodo wasn't sure she liked it.

Eula Mae returned and placed Rupert's dish carefully on the table. Eyes still on Rupert, she slid another bowl in front of Dodo.

"Where's Clyde?" Dodo asked.

Eula Mae brushed an arm across her brow. "He had somethin' to finish off for me at home. He'll be by when he's done but I hope it's soon as I'm run off my feet. Even folks in shock gotta eat."

"Do you really think any of these security guys could really work for Rigatti?" Dodo asked.

Eula Mae dragged her gaze away from Rupert and settled on Dodo. "Sure do. Money talks and buys loyalty. Rigatti's been comin' around here botherin' Lulu for months. Perfect way to dig his nose in, ain't it? I told Lulu, just agree to sell his liquor. Not like the police are going to care and it's better 'an losing everythin', but she's more stubborn than my pa's old mule. She hates to let a man push her around."

Kid came to the doorway that led to the yard looking anxious, his apron covered in red sauce and gestured to Eula Mae. "Kid's back from his break. I'd best go," she said. "With Clyde not here, I'm busier than a moth in a mitten. See y'all." She minced her way across the almost empty dance floor.

Dodo considered the hefty men standing around the edges of the club. *Were they alert to strangers and suspicious activity? Were they indeed patsies of Rigatti?* She pushed the gumbo around the bowl with her spoon.

A different band took the stage. The singer was homely and short, but his voice was like water bubbling over rocks. The new band kept the sober mood by playing ballads.

When Rupert had finished his meal, she suggested they go out to the patio. It was getting stuffy in the club and besides, she wanted to see how Lucille was doing.

The yard was full of people discussing the bombing, making it hard to find a seat. Finally, spotting a small table for two on the edge near the kitchen, she scanned the crowd for Lucille. She was absent. Beau was not there either. As she searched, Dodo noticed Cy and Dex, the other members of Lucille's band, arriving at the entrance. She waved. They wandered over to her table and pulled up two chairs.

"Mizz Dodo," they said together, Dex's smile taking over his whole face. "Mr. Rupert."

They all shook hands.

"Apart from the crazy bombin', how you likin' my hometown? Bit different from yours." Dex smacked his knee and guffawed.

"I can see why you like it so much," she said with a smile. "And the food is amazing."

The pure Southern man beamed with pride. "I'd like to take you to see my mama before you leave," he said. "I told her all about you and your fancy dresses."

"I'd be honored," she replied.

"And how are you, Cy?" she continued.

"Better than old Frankie down at *Hurdy's*," he said with a grimace. "What *is* the world coming to?"

Dodo put a hand over his. "I know. It's awful. Lucille's incredibly shaken. Is Frankie a friend of yours?"

"Third cousin." He struck his chest with a fist. "Hits me right here. I'd like to take that Rigatti and punch his lights out."

"Now, now," said Dex looking over his shoulder. "Rigatti could have spies planted all over this place who're looking for any excuse to blow *this* place to high heaven."

"I ain't scared 'a him. No sir." Cy spat on the ground.

"That may be true, but you don't want to give him an excuse to ruin Lulu, now, do ya?" said Dex.

"I suppose so."

"Where *is* Lulu?" asked Dodo. "I haven't seen her tonight."

"'Spect she's up in her apartment," speculated Dex. "She's so torn up she can't sing."

41

Cy looked behind him and into the kitchen. "Where's that Clyde?"

"Eula Mae said he'd be over later. Something about finishing up some work for her at home," said Rupert.

"That sweet boy is so good to her," said Dex with a slow smile. "Heart 'a gold. He'd do anything for his mama."

Beau appeared, filling the entrance to the patio as a young boy wearing ragged trousers pushed past him and ran into the middle of the yard, eyes wild, searching for someone. "Where's Eula Mae?"

She appeared in the doorway to the kitchen, brushing hair out of her eyes with a hand and holding a tray full of steaming bowls with the other.

"Buddy! Here I am!" she cried.

The boy ran over. "Mizz Eula Mae. It's Clyde. He won't wake up!"

The bowls full of gumbo smashed to the ground.

Chapter 6

"That boy!" cried Eula Mae, her features rigid, as everyone stopped and stared. The messenger boy hopped from one foot to another. "He can sleep through any thunderstorm, I swear." She began to take off her apron. "I don't care how old he is, I'll tan his hide. He was supposed to be staining my dining table."

Eula Mae, riled up and angry, was sure her son was just being lazy, but from what Dodo had learned about him, she wasn't so sure.

An ominous feeling overshadowed Dodo.

"I tried to poke him awake, Mizz Eula Mae, but he wouldn't stir. I think he might be ailin'."

"'Ailin? That boy ain't never sick." She tipped her head. "Cy, you tell Lulu I'll be right back."

"Sho' thing, Eula Mae."

Dodo poked Rupert in the ribs.

"We can accompany you," he said. "Not safe for a woman to be walking alone in the streets this late at night."

She gave him the side eye. "I live barely a block away, honey. I'll be back in less than five minutes. Y'all will see."

The patio was still silent.

"I'd love to see where you live," said Dodo, desperate for a reason to go with the woman.

Eula Mae eyeballed her with contempt. "At this time of night? Whatever. Keep up." She walked so fast, Dodo was practically running to keep pace.

The streets were still alive, busy with cars trolling the road, people hanging out on corners. In spite of the tragedy of the previous night, the city had rebounded and there was a festive air.

She and Rupert rounded a corner and bumped into the back of Eula Mae as she stopped abruptly outside a three story, neat, row of brightly colored houses. Her door was third from the end.

"Not as nice as Lulu's," Eula Mae informed them as she pushed the key into the lock. "But Lulu does me well and pays me fairly. It's a far cry from where we both grew up. I owe her a lot."

She pushed in, releasing a cloud of lemon polish, cigarette smoke and the strong bite of wood varnish.

"Clyde! Clyde!" Eula Mae stalked through to the kitchen and Dodo saw over her shoulder that Clyde was face down on the table, the staining cloth still in his hand.

She caught her breath and grabbed Rupert's arm.

Eula Mae tutted, rounding the table. "This ain't no time for a nap, son." She roughly shook his shoulders and in one fluid movement he slipped from the chair to the floor. Eula Mae let out an ear-piercing scream, hands slapped to her cheeks. Dodo rushed to gather the grieving mother in her arms while Rupert checked Clyde for a pulse.

He shook his head.

"Noooo!" Great waves of grief wracked Eula Mae's chest.

Dodo had never heard anything quite like it. The grief of a thousand years of a thousand mothers, all rolled into one heart-stopping wail, striking Dodo straight through the heart.

She wrestled Eula Mae into the front parlor while the distressed mother howled and moaned in abject agony. Rupert poked his head around the door. "I'll run back to the club and let Lucille know and send someone for a doctor."

Eula Mae began to struggle to her feet but Dodo gently pulled her back. "Let's wait for the doctor."

"But my boy, he might just be sick. I need to help him."

Dodo covered the hand that was pushing on the arm of the chair, with her own. "He's never going to be in pain anymore, Eula Mae."

44

Eula Mae stared with hectic eyes toward the kitchen then threw back her head and bawled some more, wringing Dodo's heart in the process.

Come on Rupert! Come on!

She held the weeping woman, ears alert for any sound.

Finally, the clatter of hurried steps echoed outside followed by several people pushing into the narrow hall.

"Eula Mae!"

"In here, Lucille," cried Dodo as other footsteps filed past into the kitchen.

The two women fell into each other in a sacred moment and Dodo felt like a trespasser. Slipping out of the room unnoticed, she made her way to the kitchen where Beau and Rupert were examining the body.

"Dodo! Come and look," said Rupert keeping his voice low. "It's harder to tell on darker skin but it looks like strangulation. What do you think?"

Dodo crouched beside the body and stared at the subtle, purple bruises blooming on the young man's neck like a macabre necklace. "Hmm," she murmured. "I wouldn't be surprised if you can see an imprint of the fingers in better light. The general impression is of large fingers though. She moved her attention to Clyde's open eyes. "Look here, his eyes are bulging and if you inspect closely, you can see pin dots of blood. A doctor would need to confirm it, of course, but this certainly bears the hallmarks of strangulation." She looked up at Beau whose face was etched with sadness. "Did someone call a doctor?"

"I sent one of our regulars from the club but don't hold your breath," he sighed. "Prohibition might be in force but our Benevolent Society doctor brews his own moonshine and is senseless most nights."

"What about the police?" she asked.

"I called them on the telephone in the club, but they aren't too reliable neither."

45

A noise from the door made Dodo look up. Lucille was holding Eula Mae, both of them riveted to the spot, gaping at Clyde. Eula Mae put out a trembling hand with a moan.

"You can spend all the time you need with him after the doctor and police have been," explained Dodo, gently. "But we need to make sure nothing gets moved that might help us find out who did this."

Lucille led the woman back to the parlor, bent over like birches in a storm.

Time for detecting.

Dodo searched the table. Clyde had almost finished staining the large piece of furniture and the sharp smell of the stain still hung in the air. If they were lucky, the murderer got some of the stain on his clothes. The open pot was still on the table.

Dodo dropped back down to the body. If the police were as incompetent as Beau believed, it was important to do her own, thorough inventory before they arrived. She re-examined the dead boy's whole neck and, pulling the body a quarter turn toward her, found a smudge of stain on the nape of his neck, just under the collar. She glanced at his fingers. They were covered in wood varnish. Of course, he could have scratched his neck at any time that night and made the mark, but it was more likely made by the murderer. She noted a couple of fresh scuffs on the kitchen floor beneath the table which Clyde would have made as he resisted the pressure.

Had Clyde known the killer and shouted to let himself in through the back door or did Clyde get up to open the front door? Either way there were no real signs of a struggle which indicated that he knew his killer and was not afraid of him.

Examining the tabletop, she observed two drops of stain. It could have spilled out as Clyde kicked his feet.

Dodo left the kitchen and walked to the front door. Examining the frame, she found no stain marks. She walked back through the kitchen and down a short hallway to a back door. *A bloodlike smudge on the frame.* She got closer. *Not blood, stain.* So, maybe Clyde had let in someone he knew through the back door, transferring the stain from his fingers to the door frame, then settling back to his task, or the killer got stain on their fingers and left the smudge as they bolted. It was a good place to start.

She opened the door, careful not to touch the handle, and looked out. Pitch dark. Finding a light switch, she succeeded in lighting up the backyard but found nothing useful.

She walked past Beau and Rupert, leaving them to guard the body and entered the parlor. Lucille appeared to be close to a breakdown.

"Mizz Dorchester here is a fine detective, Eula Mae. She helped solve Lonnie's passing. I believe she can do the same for Clyde."

Eula Mae's tear-stained face contorted with confusion. "He didn't die of natural causes? You mean, someone *killed* my sweet baby?" She yowled some more and Dodo and Lucille looked on in pained silence.

A knock at the door was as welcome as an oasis in the desert. Dodo went to answer it.

A haggard man in his late fifties stood swaying on the stoop. "Dr. Fossey." He lifted a battered hat from his head and stepped unsteadily into the hallway, leaning against a wall for support and staring at her with undisguised surprise.

"Dorothea Dorchester. A friend of Miss Lucille Bassett. Please, come this way."

Staggering down the hall to the kitchen, fumes of hard alcohol rippled from him, catching in Dodo's throat.

"Howdy," he muttered to Beau and Rupert before snapping his head up to peer at the unexpected white man in Eula Mae's kitchen.

"He's at this here side of the table, Mac," said Beau with contemptuous familiarity.

The doctor put a hand on the table to brace himself and shuffled to the other side. With a groan he put the other hand to his heart and slurred, "Well, bless my soul. Clyde. Who'd a done such a thing?"

No one answered as the inebriated man fell to one knee with a grunt and ran his hands over Clyde's still neck to feel for a pulse.

"Dead alright," he confirmed. "I'll fill out a death certificate." He made to stand up.

Horrified, Dodo gasped, "Doctor, I'm sure you noticed the bruising on his neck?"

Dr. Fossey let gravity pull him back down. "Ah, of course, let's see…hmmm, don't like them bruises. Na-huh." He retrieved a small flashlight from his pocket and shone them into Clyde's blank eyes. "Hmm." He rolled the corpse over then let it fall back and scrambled to his feet.

"Death by strangulation. Cut and dry. I'll fill out the paperwork and file it with the city in the morning. Now, if you'll excuse me, I'll be a goin'."

Shocked into silence by the unprofessionalism of his manner, Dodo stood with hands on her hips. Upon hearing the front door close, Beau blew air through his teeth. "Used to be a good doctor but he let the drink get the better 'o him. He's drunk most days, now. Complete waste of talent."

Dodo realized that Dr. Fossey hadn't even stopped in to offer condolences to Eula Mae.

Another knock.

"I'll get it," said Beau.

Alone in the kitchen, Dodo saw anger flash across Rupert's features. "What a complete farce. I've seen better medicine practiced by a goat!"

48

"The man could barely stand up let alone do his job. But all we need is his confirmation of the manner of death, which he provided," said Dodo.

"I suppose, but I should hate to have to call him if I were ill."

"Me too!" agreed Dodo, thinking of her no-nonsense, uptight doctor in Harley Street.

The crunch of large boots thundered in the hall and four policemen entered the kitchen; three in uniform and one in a light colored suit, a cigarette hanging from his bottom lip.

His baggy eyes perked up at the sight of Rupert and Dodo. Then a frown clouded his rough, sun-weathered features. "You friends of the deceased? Where's Eula Mae?"

"We're friends of Lucille Basset, actually," said Dodo.

"That right?" murmured the policeman, addressing the words to Rupert.

"We're here for the memorial service," she explained.

"Ah." The ash at the end of the cigarette plunged toward the floor, saved by his wrinkled jacket. Sweeping it off with a hand, he made no attempt to clean it from Eula Mae's spotless floor.

Dodo took an instant dislike to the rude man.

"Now, what do we have here?" His tone was as emotionless as his bland features. He bent over and harshly fingered Clyde's young neck. "Strangled. That what the doc said?" Straightening he looked at Beau. "You the first to find him?"

"No," he responded. "Eula Mae sent a messenger to see what was taking Clyde so long to get to work."

The policeman screwed up an eye. "Name?"

"Buddy Goodman," offered Beau. "He's about eleven."

"Oh, I know 'im," said the policeman. "Always gettin' in trouble. I'll need to talk to 'im. Could be he's the murderer."

49

The idea was utterly preposterous! Even an idiot could see that the bruises were made by an adult. What was the man thinking?

The policeman arched a bushy brow. "Why are you all here in the house?"

"Buddy thought Clyde was merely sick. We couldn't have his mother running around the streets this late, so we accompanied her," explained Rupert.

The crass policeman, who still hadn't offered his name, dropped his chin in disbelief, then chuckled. "A proper gentleman and no mistakin'!" It was not pronounced as a compliment.

Dodo was still fuming at the man's ineptitude and wondered if he had been given the position by the workings of Rigatti because he didn't seem to have a rational thought in his head. She thought it prudent to let Rupert do the talking. She communicated this to Rupert with a look.

"It was obvious to us, from the moment we saw Clyde slumped on the table, that he was dead," explained Rupert.

The policeman screwed up his lips so that the obnoxious cigarette was touching his nose. "Obvious? How?"

"His prone position on the table when we first arrived, and then we checked for the rise and fall of his back. His mother was sure he was just being lazy and went to shake him awake. That's when the body fell to the floor and I checked for a pulse."

The officer stroked his broad chin. "He was sitting at the table when you found him?"

"Slumped over actually," corrected Rupert.

Dodo tipped her head at Rupert twice and pointed to her neck as Eula Mae's sobs penetrated the hall and made their way into the kitchen.

"Oh, and then we saw the large bruises. On his neck," finished Rupert.

The officer narrowed his eyes.

"What're *you* doing here, Buckley?" It was as if the officer had forgotten the huge man's presence.

Strange that Beau was letting Rupert do all the talking.

"Badger," said Beau carefully. "Eula Mae is Lucille's best friend. Soon as we learned that Clyde was—had passed, I ran here with Lucille. She's in the other room with Eula Mae."

"*Lieutenant* Badger to you, Buckley," he sneered through pale, cracked lips. "So, you and Lucille were at the club?"

"Yessir."

Dodo had a flashback of Beau arriving just as the boy Buddy delivered his message. Where had he been before that?

Badger's bleary eyes swept the room in a cursory fashion. "What's that confounded smell?"

"Wood stain," said Dodo, resisting the urge to roll her eyes at the inspector's lack of perception.

He snapped his eyes to Dodo. "That so? You do a lot of wood workin', little lady?"

She pointed to the small can of stain on the table. "It's open and Clyde had a staining cloth in his hand when he was slouched over." *Not exactly a mystery.*

Badger dragged a stubby finger over the tabletop and Dodo hoped he would get stain all over it. However, though the table was still sticky, when he examined his finger, it was clean.

Was it even worth telling this horrid, boar of a man about the smudge on the back door frame and the one on Clyde's neck? Given his antipathy she didn't think so. He could find them himself. It was his job, after all.

Badger clapped his hands. "Right. I think I've seen all I need to see. Let's go, boys."

Dodo balked. *He's not even going to* pretend *to do his job!*

The three of them watched in stunned silence as the policemen left the room and then the house. Like the doctor, they didn't even have the courtesy to stop and see the victim's mother.

Dodo threw her arms in the air as the front door latched closed. "What was that? I've never seen such shoddy, bally police work in my life!"

Beau quirked a brow. "Honestly, y'all, I'm surprised he came at all and didn't just send his minions. Unless you line his pocket, he's not disposed to do much in the way of detecting."

Shaking her head in disgust, Dodo declared, "Then *I* will make sure justice is served. I will have to find the killer myself."

Chapter 7

"This is all my fault," said Lucille, holding Eula Mae close. "It's a warning to me like the bombing was to Frankie, over at the *Hurdy Gurdy*. Rigatti did this to strong-arm me into signing on with him. If I'd just toed the line, Clyde would still be alive."

"Unfortunately, that *is* a reasonable conclusion," Dodo agreed. "But in this case, I don't think it's likely."

Lucille's features gathered thunder.

"But it's a good place to start." Dodo paused a beat then asked Eula Mae, "Putting the gangsters aside, did Clyde have any enemies?"

"No!" Eula Mae rushed to answer before Dodo had even finished the sentence. "He was a good boy."

"I'm not saying he wasn't," said Dodo gently. "But people have faults and arguments happen, grudges are held. Things like that."

Eula Mae's lips puckered. "There was a kid two blocks over, used to give Clyde a hard time at school. Clyde used to stutter, and people made fun of him. Actually, kids were always makin' fun of him. Near on broke my heart. I told him just to ignore them, but who knows? Maybe he fought back a time or two."

"That's good," encouraged Dodo. "What is his name?"

"Everyone calls him Bubba, but his name is William Swanson."

"Anyone else?" prodded Dodo.

She dabbed at her eyes with a soaked handkerchief. "No one I can think of."

"Well, if someone does come to mind, you know where to find me." She placed a hand on Eula Mae's shoulder. "Lucille, can we have a word?"

Lucille closed her eyes and nodded. "Will you be okay, sugar?"

"I'll stay with her," offered Beau. Lucille's face filled with an appreciation that needed no words.

Dodo and Lucille went into the hall, closing the door to the parlor.

"Do you really think Rigatti is responsible?" began Dodo. "Strangulation seems too quiet for a man like him. The bombing was a massive attack on an empty building that got everyone's attention. Shooting into a crowd of people as he drives by hoping he hits someone also seems more his style. But this is more personal. Like Clyde was the intended target, not collateral damage. Do you see what I'm getting at?"

Lucille chewed her cheek. "I do. But Rigatti has no respect for human life if it gets in his way. He has the blood of dozens on his hands. What's one more?"

"I know you want it to be him," said Dodo. "But if we put Rigatti aside for a minute, can you think of anyone else? Like this Bubba?"

"Bubba's a bully, for sure, and even as an adult he knocks his missus around, but I don't see him as a killer."

Dodo tried to come at the questions from a different angle. "Sometimes people are killed because they witnessed a crime or know too much. Could that be the case here?"

"I don't know how? Clyde's intellect... , well, he's like a child. But don't go thinkin' Eula Mae treats him like a baby. When he's not working, his time is his own, pretty much. She doesn't ask for an accountin' of every minute."

"What about at work. Waiters can overhear things," Dodo suggested.

"No idea. Never told me if he did."

"Well, mull it over," said Dodo. "Could it be that he saw something he shouldn't have or someone coming out of the wrong house of a morning or some such? Maybe ask Eula Mae to think about it too."

54

Lucille's black eyes glistened. "I will." She took a shaky breath. "That boy was his mother's reason for living."

Dodo took a chance. "Could his…father have any reason to…you know?"

Lucille threw back her shoulders. "No! Thankfully, that brute is already six feet under."

"Well, that's one suspect off the list. Now, with your permission, I'll see if the neighbors saw anything. I didn't get the impression Lieutenant Badger was going to give this too much of his precious time."

"You got that right, sugar! He only protects Rigatti's interests. And if it has nothing to do with Rigatti's empire, he has no stake in it." She wiped her cheek. "And I most certainly *do* want you to investigate." She glanced at her watch. "But it's past one in the morning and Eula Mae's neighbors are respectable folk. They'll be in bed. You go on home. I'll stay with Eula Mae and help her make arrangements for tomorrow."

"If it's all the same to you, I'll just take one more look in the kitchen before I head back," Dodo responded.

"Suit yourself." Lucille slipped back into the parlor.

The kitchen was empty except for the corpse. A deathly silence filled the void. It did not look like the lieutenant would collect the body to perform an autopsy.

She stood behind the chair Clyde had been sitting in and mimed staining the table. She imagined someone coming to the back door. Would they just walk in? Did people here lock their doors at night? In English villages back doors were often kept unlocked.

A narrow corridor led out of the kitchen to the back door. Hooks lined the wall and various aprons and light coats hung from them. Well-worn shoes were lined up beneath as if waiting for Clyde to step into them. The door was half-mottled glass. Someone standing on the other side would have been distorted but if the person was familiar, would they be recognizable? And it was dark. Probably not.

She examined the smudge for any kind of fingerprint. None.

Hearing a noise, she walked back the few steps to the kitchen. Rupert.

"Can you do me a favor?" she asked.

"Ready and willing," he said with that smile, stepping over the body. They really should get a sheet.

"Pop out this door. I want to see if I can recognize you."

Rupert followed her and stepped outside into the dark, nose to the glass door. Dodo could see a vague figure and even though he was as dear to her as anyone on earth, she could hardly tell if he were male or female.

"Is there a knocker or a bell?" she called.

A moment passed. "Not one that I can see," Rupert replied.

Dodo opened the door and let him back in.

"I have to verify this because I don't know the culture here, but I bet they keep their back doors unlocked. Would the killer have just walked in, or would they have opened the door and called out?"

"If the door was unlocked, my guess is that the murderer slithered in as quietly as possible and took Clyde by surprise while he sat at the table," said Rupert.

"It might seem that way, except look." She pointed to the smudge of stain on the door frame.

"How long have they been working on this table?" Rupert asked. "The smudge could have got there yesterday."

Dodo jutted out her bottom lip, blowing air through her hair. "Dash it! You're right."

They walked back into the kitchen and she took up her position by the chair, careful not to touch the body, and mimed staining the table again. The passageway to the door was in front of her.

"I'm right! No one could sneak in without him seeing as he was facing the hallway."

"So you are, darling."

"Perhaps the person knocked. Clyde gets up." She moved back, holding her imaginary cloth. "He goes to the door. Since the murder did not take place in the hall, he must have recognized the person and not felt threatened. He probably had the killer go in front of him, or again, the murder could have taken place in the hall. Then he was comfortable enough to go back to staining so he could get to work at the club. It was then the killer struck."

"What if it's like England? Back door friends let themselves in and call out," said Rupert.

"Same thing. It's someone he knows and isn't frightened of—which rules out Rigatti or his thugs in my opinion. Clyde keeps working and they wander behind him and, bam!" She tipped her head. "I wonder if the neighbors heard anything since they share walls."

"Your theory assumes that the person came here with the aim of murder," said Rupert. "What if they came to reason with him and Clyde refused to comply?"

"I did think of that, but there's no sign of a struggle except the scuff marks under the table." She tapped her finger to her lips. "It suggests that Clyde was at ease in the killer's presence and was taken quite by surprise."

It wasn't much to go on. She stifled a yawn. "Let's get some sleep and interview the neighbors bright and early. I really hope they saw or heard something."

Chapter 8

After a fitful night and a rushed breakfast, Rupert and Dodo left to question Eula Mae's neighbors. Before knocking on the first door, Dodo worried the homeowner might be annoyed at being questioned twice. Then she chuckled to herself. *No! Badger wouldn't have bothered interviewing them at all.*

At the house to the right of Eula Mae's, a tiny, elderly woman wearing a multicolored scarf around her hair, opened the door. Upon seeing two, well-to-do, white people, her eyes flashed wide.

"This 'bout the bizzness next door?"

Dodo nodded. "Why, yes. Please excuse the intrusion but Miss Bassett has hired us to investigate poor Clyde's death. May we come in?"

The woman stood back to let them pass, then looked out and down the street to see if anyone was looking. The house was the same floorplan as Eula Mae's but the entryway was painted a sultry, dark purple.

They followed the spry, little lady into her front parlor. A tasteful mix of yellow and peacock blue, there were pictures of children on every available surface. A cigarette was sitting in an ash tray, but she stubbed it out.

"Sit yo'selves down. I'd heard there was an English woman in town. Now I get to see you for myself! Can I get you some iced tea?"

The very thought of it made Dodo's teeth ache. "That's very kind of you but we've just had breakfast." Dodo smoothed her skirt. "I apologize for coming so early and if you've been questioned by the police already—"

"That good for nothing Badger ain't been by to see me!" she interrupted, as she crossed her arms over her chest. "Nor is 'e likely too!"

As Dodo had predicted.

"Thank you so much for seeing us, Mrs.—?"

"You just call me Mizz Minnie." She adjusted the bright scarf around a face as lined as a topographical map. It was obvious to Dodo that Minnie was trying to look as though she was not taking in every detail of her outfit.

"As I mentioned, Miss Bassett has given us authority to look into Clyde's death," said Dodo. Minnie's faded eyes grew wide and she pulled a handkerchief from the sleeve of her lilac blouse and flicked it in the air. "Ain't' she somethin', that Mizz Bassett? Mmm, mmm. She and her daddy were poor as mice when she was a baby but look at her now!" Minnie blew her nose, the noise rivaling any trumpet.

Dodo smothered a chuckle. "Indeed."

Rupert brushed his mouth to conceal a smile. "We're hoping you saw or heard something around ten o'clock last night?"

"Wish I had! Wish I had!" She shook her head, eyes still on Rupert. "I go to sleep at nine and put cotton in my ears. I got used to doin' it when my Billy was alive. He was a snorer! Lands sakes! And now I can't kick the habit." She dropped her voice and looked around as if the walls had ears. "Between that and a little moonshine, I sleep like the dead." Her eyes popped wide again and she slapped an arthritic hand across her mouth. "What a thing to say with that poor young boy lying next door." She rearranged the handkerchief and blew the roof off the room.

Dodo frowned. "The undertaker didn't come to take him away for burial?"

Minnie's frown matched Dodo's. "I can tell you folks ain't from round here. The Benevolent Society will take care of all that, don't you worry."

"And the police didn't take the body for an autopsy?"

A throaty, humorless laugh spilled from Minnie's lips. "That low down, good for nuthin' doctor won't be back. But I'm tickled that Mizz Bassett got you on the case. You some kind of private investigator? Maybe that boy will get somethin' like justice."

"Something like that," said Dodo. "I've been involved in quite a few cases."

"That so? You don't look like one." Minnie shifted to the edge of her chair and pinned Rupert with her stare. "Where you from, sugar?"

"Uh, London." Rupert squirmed a little in his seat at her directness.

"You look like them stars in them movies. I ain't never seen peepers that blue before." She grinned exposing slightly blackened teeth. Dodo was sure it was from the cigarettes and sugary tea.

"I have my mother's eyes," Rupert explained.

Time to get back to business.

"Has anything unusual happened here over the last few days or so?" Dodo asked.

"The milkman ran off with Mizz Lila." Minnie grinned. "But I'm sure that's not the kind of thing you mean."

"Not really," said Dodo wondering if this was all a colossal waste of time.

Minnie straightened and slapped the arm of her chair. "Someone painted 'rat' on Mizz Eula Mae's front door yesterday, but dear Clyde washed it off before his mama saw it."

Dodo's gut clenched. "Do you know what it meant?"

Minnie twisted her wrinkled lips and shook her head. "Meant someone thought he had snitched on them, I 'spose, but I don't think that's likely. He was a good boy with a child's innocent mind."

Dodo's hopes rose. This could be the key to the whole murder.

"I don't suppose you happened to see who painted it?" she asked.

"Eula Mae and Clyde get home late from the club, and I get up early. I'd say that ugly deed was done around four or five 'o clock in the morning since they didn't see it when they got home but it was there by the time I was up. Shocking!"

Leaning forward Dodo asked, "Do you have an idea of who may have done it?"

Minnie sighed and clasped her hands on her knees. "There are good, church going folk in this city and then there are the others, the ones who deal in the vices. This 'ere place is full of 'em. They'd kill as easy as eat sugar pie." She raised a brow. "I'd say you got your work cut out for you, little lady."

As Dodo and Rupert stood on the doorstep on the other side of Eula Mae's house, Dodo tipped her head and said, "I think you have a fan in that one."

Rupert ignored her comment. "That's something, isn't it? The threat on the door."

"It certainly shows someone had a grievance with the family. But if no one saw who did it, I'm not sure the knowledge will help us much. Fingers crossed!"

She knocked on the bright blue, front door.

At first, it appeared that no one was home. However, as they were about to leave, a middle-aged woman wearing a pink mob cap appeared, holding a tortoiseshell cat. Peering at them through thick glasses as if they were a curiosity in a museum, she whispered, "What can I do for you folks?"

Dodo took the lead. "You may have heard that your neighbor was killed last night."

The woman's free hand slammed to her chest. "Have mercy! That's why I didn't want to open the door. I'm nervous as a long-tailed cat in a room full of rocking chairs." She beckoned to them. "Come in! Come in!"

Following the pattern of Minnie, she hurried them into her hall then looked up and down the street to make sure no one was looking. Her entryway was painted a happy

61

primrose yellow. She shooed them with her hands toward the parlor and dropped the cat on the entry floor. Iridescent abstract art hung on dark blue walls and a picture of a man playing a saxophone sat on an upright piano.

Once seated, her eyes flew between Dodo and Rupert. "Eula Mae told me all about the pretty English lady and her fine clothes. So, what's the scoop?"

"We were hoping you could tell us," Dodo responded.

The woman shrank, blending into her seat. Well, *I* don't know nothin'."

Dodo checked her disappointment. "Perhaps you know more than you think—"

"Mizz Frannie."

"Miss Bassett has asked us to look into the...unfortunate incident."

"That Mizz Bassett, she's a saint. She helped Eula Mae get her place." She ran a finger along the arm of her chair. "I'm lucky too. My Bennie plays the saxophone in one a' them jazz joints—not Mizz Bassett's. He makes good money."

Perhaps being less direct was the ticket with Miss Frannie.

"Is that your husband playing the saxophone?" Dodo asked pointing to the photograph.

"Yes. That was taken about ten years ago now." Frannie's face relaxed.

"He's a very handsome man," Dodo added.

"Still is. Count my lucky stars every day."

"Have you been neighbors with Eula Mae long?"

"She moved in after us. We came to this house over ten years ago—'bout the time that photograph was taken. I thought I'd died and gone to heaven, you know. My mama didn't like Bennie, no ma'am. Said he was as welcome as an outhouse breeze and that playin' the saxophone wasn't a *real* job. She told me we'd end up in the poor house. But look at us now."

Dodo had an idea. "Does the club your husband plays for sell alcohol?"

Frannie's eyes narrowed to slits. "You with the police?"

"I assure you we are not. Like I said, Miss Bassett has asked us to investigate Clyde's death."

Frannie cradled her round face in both hands. "Such a sweet boy. Not a hoodlum like those other fellas, always gettin' into trouble. No, sir. The good Lord put a veil over Clyde's mind so he weren't tempted to join those gangs. He always had a kind word for Mizz Priss—my cat. And if he was cleanin' their stoop, he'd sweep mine too. Such a comfort to his mother and now to be torn from her like this—it's criminal, that's what it is."

"On that count we agree with you one hundred per cent," said Dodo. "Mizz Minnie said she saw some graffiti on their door a few days ago. I don't suppose you saw it or who did it?"

"I saw that boy washing it off afore his mother got up. This city is descending into chaos, I tell you. That's why I don't go out in the evenin's and pray to the good Lord for my Bennie every night."

Dodo was glad the conversation had circled back to Frannie's husband. "You didn't say if the club where he works sells spirits."

Dodo could almost hear the shackles rise. "What if it does?"

"Perhaps Mr. Rigatti compelled them to sell his product?" Dodo suggested.

Frannie rested her chin on her fist. "It's clear you aren't from round here, honey. That Rigatti runs this whole blessed town. He might just as well sit there in city hall in the mayor's chair since he's the one that pulls the strings. I know you heard about the bombin'. That's what happens when you say no to Rigatti."

"Do you think Clyde's murder had anything to do with Rigatti and Mizz Bassett's club?"

Frannie sucked in her plump cheeks. "I put any murder round here right at Rigatti's doorstep. That crook could crawl under a snake's belly. No conscience. Kills like it's as easy as eating Sunday dinner."

"Are you aware that Miss Bassett has so far refused Rigatti's invitations?" added Rupert. "Do you think he would strike out at her employees to send her a message?"

"Wouldn't put it past him," said Frannie, one eye almost shut. "I know he has musicians at several clubs on his payroll."

"Is that so?" commented Dodo.

"That's how that scum works; outside *and* inside pressure. So far, my Bennie has resisted but when your family is threatened..." Her hands began to shake as she flattened the full apron that covered her dress.

"Have you been threatened?" asked Rupert scooting forward in his seat.

"That's not what I said. If you think I implied that— well, I didn't mean to suggest..." The muscles in her jaw tightened.

If Frannie was frightened, she was not about to reveal anything incriminating. Dodo needed to steer the conversation away from Rigatti. "Going back to Clyde. Did you talk to him while he was washing the paint off the front door?"

"I was leavin' to get some groceries at the *Piggly Wiggly* when I saw him. I asked what in tarnation he was doin'. Thought he was *paintin'* the door. He explained what happened and that he wanted to get it off before his mama woke and saw it. He begged me not to tell her."

"Did he seem nervous?"

"He was muttering somethin' as he worked and looking over his shoulder, but I couldn't make out what he was saying," she replied.

"Did he have any idea who had done it?"

Frannie's mouth shrugged. "I asked, but I could barely get another word out of him."

This behavior indicated that Clyde was angry and anxious. She wondered if *he* knew exactly who had painted the offensive word on his mother's door.

"Did you see anyone unusual around here in the days leading up to the killing?"

Tapping her chin, Frannie suddenly said, "A fella I didn't know was washing Eula Mae's windows yesterday. I thought it strange 'cause it was almost dark and Clyde washes their windows and mine. But Mizz Priss had got out and I was runnin' up the road after her before she got hit by one of them cars. My heart was a'flutterin' and by the time I caught up with her I was flat out a' breath. Brought her back and made myself a drink to calm down. She's my baby, you see."

The only pictures in the room were of Bennie and his band. No children or grandchildren.

"Could you describe the man?" asked Dodo.

"Tall. 'Bout thirty or so, I reckon. But it was dark and he was up the ladder and I was all about Mizz Priss."

"Well, it's something for us to follow up on." Dodo thought about taking her leave when she remembered something. "Miss Frannie, do all your neighbors keep their back doors unlocked?"

Frannie's chin dropped. "I used to, but not these days…"

"Eula Mae's back door was unlocked last night."

"Don't surprise me none. Eula Mae is too trusting."

"Did everyone *know* her door was always unlocked?"

"Weren't no secret, though my Bennie told her a thousand times, a single lady should lock her doors. She always told him she had Clyde…" her voice cracked.

"You've been most helpful," said Dodo, standing.

Frannie opened the parlor door to reveal Mizz Priss preening on the stairs. Frannie tucked the cat under her arm and opened the front door just as the postman was getting ready to knock.

Frannie slapped her forehead. "Morning, Jerry. You gave me a package yesterday, but it was for Mizz Eula Mae."

Jerry was busy staring at Dodo and Rupert. "What now?"

"I said, you gave me a package addressed to Mizz Eula Mae."

He shrugged. "I'm only human, Mizz Frannie, like the good Lord made me. I makes mistakes."

Frannie addressed Dodo. "I took it over and gave it to Clyde as his mama was out. It was flat like it had photographs in it. Perhaps you saw it?"

They certainly had not.

Chapter 9

Though everyone was eager for gossip, none of the other neighbors had anything to add to Frannie and Minnie's testimonies.

"Let's find out what was in that package," said Dodo, checking her watch.

They let themselves into the back of Eula Mae's house and were jolted at the crush of people cramming into her modest home. In addition, a string of people were waiting in a line offering baked goods and condolences. Casseroles were piled high on the unfinished table and pie dresser. Dodo went up on her toes but could see neither Eula Mae nor Lucille in the kitchen. She and Rupert edged their way past the queue, until they reached the parlor which was also crawling with humanity.

Dodo caught Lucille's eye and tipped her head. Lucille squeezed Eula Mae's hand then forced herself through the crowd and into the congested front hall.

"I liked it better when you two were the talk of the town," murmured Lucille struggling to smile, but failing.

"Is there somewhere quieter we can go?" asked Dodo.

"Follow me." Lucille headed up the stairs and into a dainty, bright bedroom with a brass bed and colorful, quilted counterpane. Pictures of Clyde at various ages dotted the room. Lucille sat on the end of the bed, a wet and twisted handkerchief in her hand.

"What's up?"

"Just a couple of things," began Dodo. "The boy that found him, Buddy Goodman. Why was he the one sent?"

"Buddy hangs around the club waiting to run errands. He's proved surprisingly dependable over the last six months so I keep him around—and I know his mother could do with any extra money."

"Where can we find him?"

Lucille wiped her nose with the wet cloth. "He lives on Royal, just the other side of Canal, downtown. Let me send Beau with you."

"Thank you. And the neighbor, Frannie, said she received a flat package mistakenly delivered to her that was meant for Eula Mae. I was wondering what was in it?"

"I'll ask her when we send everyone home." Lucille brushed her cheek with her fingers.

"Who *are* all these people?" Rupert asked.

"Friends, neighbors, and the Benevolent Society ladies. This is expected after someone passes away," Lucille explained. "The Benevolent Society ladies will help Eula Mae with the funeral costs and arrangements."

Dodo drew the conclusion that the Benevolent Society here in New Orleans was similar to the ones in England.

"By the way, your opinion of the police is shared by Eula Mae's neighbors," added Rupert.

"It's accepted by the whole blessed town. We just know that calling the police is not going to do us much good."

Nervous that what she was about to say might disturb Lucille more, Dodo tried to make her tone as gentle as possible. "Were you aware that someone had scrawled 'rat' on Eula Mae's front door yesterday morning?"

Lucille's head snapped up. "What! No! Why didn't Eula Mae tell me?"

"Because she didn't know. Clyde saw it early and made sure to clean it off before she woke up. He didn't want to worry her."

Lucille started to tear at the handkerchief, gold bangles jingling. "Do you think it has something to do with this?"

"Too early to tell, but we'll follow up on it," Dodo assured her.

Lucille nodded.

"You probably already know that Frannie's husband works for a club that's controlled by Rigatti. She seems pretty nervous about it."

"She should be," replied Lucille. "Rigatti is a vicious, violent man. Not to mention the bombing and the murder have everyone on edge."

Dodo continued, "She also told us the weirdest thing—someone was washing Eula Mae's windows…at dusk."

"What the—?"

"I know. It's very suspicious," said Dodo validating Lucille's concern.

The hard lines on Lucille's face softened at the edges. "You're an angel looking into this. Badger won't give it the time of day." She hugged Dodo releasing a cloud of mimosa. "Now, let me call Beau."

Crossing Canal Street was like walking into a different world, and Dodo was grateful that the hulking Beau was with them.

Children were spilling out of narrow tenement houses, some playing, some bawling. A harried mother in an apron, a baby on her hip, stepped out clipping a boy of about seven round the ear and motioning him inside.

"This is it," said Beau after they had walked a few more blocks. "Why don't I go and bring him out to you?"

"Alright," said Dodo, appreciating that their presence in Buddy's home might complicate matters.

She and Rupert stood under the shade of a large tree while Beau knocked. A cluster of young children looked up in awe at the towering man as Beau stood at the entrance to their tiny house. A thin woman, cradling a newborn, pushed her way through the children, a mixture of fear and defiance on her features. She relaxed as Beau spoke to her in low tones and eventually nodded, pointing away from the house.

Beau made his way back to them under the shelter of the tree. "He's playing toward the river."

Two blocks farther on, a group of tattered boys and girls were playing with a stick in the middle of the road. A small-boned boy with wild hair, stood at the ready, stick held high above one shoulder. A taller boy threw a ball and the batter swung the stick. *Thwack!* The ball sailed over the heads of the children in the outfield, hitting the road and rolling under a parked car.

The boy at bat, whom Dodo recognized as Buddy, high-tailed it around the bases, made from old newspapers held down with stones, lapping those already on base. With a triumphant grin, eyes sparkling, he slid on his bottom back to where he started.

Half of the group dissolved into shrieks and cheers as Beau clapped enthusiastically, shouting, "Bravo! As good a home run as I have ever seen!"

When his teammates had finished slapping his back, Buddy wandered over to where Beau, Dodo, and Rupert stood.

Shading his eyes as he looked up at Beau, white teeth shining out of an artless face, he declared, "You's Mizz Lulu's sweetheart." Then sliding his gaze over to Dodo and Rupert, he said," Howdy! I seed you t'other day. Y'all are from over yonder."

"We certainly are," replied Rupert with a chuckle.

"This 'bout Clyde?"

Beau nodded. "Mind if we have a word?"

"Sure! Games over now." He patted down his ratty trouser legs and puffed out his chest, turning back to his friends. "I've got bizz'ness with Mr. Buckley. Later alligators!"

"In a while crocodile!" yelled back his playmates.

"Is there somewhere near here we can go for a cola?" Rupert asked.

Beau pointed back over Canal Street. "Two blocks up."

"Cola! I love cola!" yelled Buddy. "Oowee! Wait till Shorty hears. He'll be fit to be tied."

They walked up the street as Buddy danced around and through them until they stopped outside a shop that said *drugstore*. Dodo frowned.

"Since Prohibition, all the drugstores have soda fountains," Beau explained. "After you." He held Buddy back while Dodo entered.

A wrinkled gentleman wearing a peaked cap and a red and white apron beamed at Dodo over the counter. "And what can I get you fine folks today?"

"A cola please," replied Dodo.

"What flavor?" All the wrinkles moved up in expectation.

"Uh, I thought..." she looked at Beau helplessly while his shoulders shook.

"Every soda is called cola. You can choose orange, lemon or actual ᶜCoca-Cola."

"ᶜCoca-Cola please," she replied.

"Me too!" cried Buddy, pushing himself up the counter with his arms.

Taking their drinks, they settled at a table by the window under a large fan that moved the stifling air. The cold soda trickled pleasantly down Dodo's throat.

Within seconds, Buddy had finished, smacking his lips.

"Buddy, can you tell me more about finding Miss Eula Mae's boy?" asked Dodo.

Her question wiped the innocent smile from his face. "I didn't know he were dead when I ran back to tell Mizz Eula Mae."

"You're not in trouble," she assured him. "We're just wondering about some of the details."

Buddy's serious, black eyes found Beau's, who nodded slightly.

Dodo continued. "When you got to the house, was the back door open?"

His little eyebrows danced a jig. "Unlocked? Yeah. Ain't everyone's?"

71

"Did you pass anyone in the street when you arrived at their house?"

His small, bottom lip jutted out as he pondered. "There was this old guy walkin' a dog. He asked me what I's doin' out so late. None 'a his bizz'ness anyway. Then a couple older kids—I hid from them so they couldn't push me around. After that, I seed two ladies all dressed up for a night on the town. It's pretty busy here at night, you know."

"That's very helpful, Buddy," she encouraged. "Now, when you went in, did you pass anyone on the back stoop or see anyone leaving the back yard?"

"No, ma'am."

"Did you knock or call out to Clyde?"

"I've run errands for Mizz Eula Mae before and I ain't never knocked. She might live uptown now but she ain't stuck up, none. But I did call out. Phew! It stunk like a skunk in there." He waved a hand in front of his little nose. "Then I seed that Clyde was paintin' the table but he'd fallen asleep. Dyin' weren't on my mind at all. I'd a been spooked if I'd a' thought he were dead. Anyways, I shakes him to wake up, but he don't. So, I thought he were sick and ran back to tell Mizz Eula Mae and she gets madder 'an a puffed toad and runs home to tan his hide."

"Didn't you notice that his eyes were open?"

"Nah, his head was turned the other way," Buddy explained.

"Was there a package in the kitchen?" she asked.

"Nope."

"Did you touch the wet table?"

His face screwed up with disgust. "No, ma'am. I didn't wanna stink."

"When you were in the kitchen, did anything seem out of place?"

Buddy took a sip through his red and white straw then remembered he had no cola left in his bottle and considered Dodo's question.

"I don't think so. But I weren't there more 'an two minutes."

"Thank you, Buddy."

He held up the empty glass. "Can I 'ave another?"

Chapter 10

After seeing Buddy home, the three of them walked back to the club.

"How long have you known Lucille?" Rupert asked Beau.

He clicked his tongue. "I'm not native to New Orleans. I was just passing through on business when I happened to stop by Lulu's club. Her daddy was alive back then." He stopped walking as if reliving the moment. "That voice, that face...I was smitten." He shook his head and continued strolling. "I had no one to go home to, no siblings and my parents were both dead. But I had a little money, so I stayed. Been ten years now."

Dodo had noticed immediately that Beau's suits were well-tailored, and his shoes were high-end with leather soles.

"What do you do?" she asked. It was a mystery to her why Lucille was so against this charming man.

Beau's handsome, round face fell into horizontal lines as a broad smile took over. "Ya'll ever heard the expression, *honey wagon*, Mizz Dor'thea?"

Confused, Dodo replied, "By the look on your face, I'm guessing it has nothing to do with bees."

"No ma'am," he responded with a low chuckle that vibrated from deep in his vast chest. "No bees." He wiggled his eyebrows and Dodo couldn't help but smile back. "As a boy in Nashville Tennessee, I collected waste from folks' pail closets. In polite society we called it 'collecting honey'." He looked hard at her to see if she understood.

"Ah." She exchanged a glance with Rupert.

"I worked hard and managed to save a little," Beau continued. "There's a lot 'a money in that there honey, and I could see that times were a-changing and folks were tired of runnin' to old-fashioned outhouses. So, I used my

74

money and started a septic tank business in Tennessee. It's not a job to everyone's taste, to be sure, but I was born with a defective sense of smell so it don't bother me none. Business boomed. I had come to New Orleens looking to expand my organization to Louisiana, when I heard Lucille sing and Cupid's arrow struck me right in the heart. That's part of her problem with me. Made my money in muck."

Dodo had never considered such an occupation, never given a second thought to where her own waste ended up. But she could sympathize with Lucille.

"Did you ever start your business here?" asked Rupert, his face showing the incredulity that Dodo felt.

"Oh, yessir! It's like gold. But Lucille's embarrassed by it. I don't hold it against her none. But the truth is, I don't have to get my hands dirty anymore. Well, hardly ever. Now, I'm just the man at the top. They call me the Honey King."

Dodo wrinkled her nose. "Hardly ever?"

"The night of poor Clyde's murder, I was called out to a job that had gone south. Took a lot of fancy talkin' to soothe *that* lady, I can tell you! Made me late to the club."

The memory of Beau arriving at the same time as Buddy that night flashed through her mind.

"Did you know Clyde well?" she asked. "What did you think of him?"

"He was just ten years old when I moved here, 'bout the same age Buddy is now. He was always a little slow, but in my opinion it meant the devil couldn't tempt him. He was a sweet chil' who never got into trouble like most boys that age. And he loved his mama. Oh, how he loved his mama." His voice faltered.

Dodo gave him a moment to regain his composure.

"And as he grew up?" she finally said.

"I'd say his mind stayed about the same age as when I first met him. His body developed but not his soul, if you get my meanin'."

"When did he begin working at *Lulu's?*"

"Oh, he was always there with his mama. Sleepin' in the kitchen when he was little, and then around fifteen he began to take out a few orders when it got busy. He was good at it and sociable—that boy never knew a stranger." His bass voice broke in a choke and he wiped his eye. Removing his hat, he placed it over his heart. "That chil' done gone straight to heaven."

Dodo sidestepped a stray dog trotting along the sidewalk. "He didn't make any enemies?"

"No ma'am. Everyone loved that boy."

Someone certainly hadn't.

They crossed the busy road, street cars clanging their bells as they passed. When they reached the other side, Dodo asked, "Do you know anything about Clyde's father?"

Beau shook his head. "Lucille and Eula Mae don't talk about him. All I know is the brute is dead and Clyde's coming into the world was from an act of violence. I asked Lulu about it once when she was in a good mood. I understand that Eula Mae tried a tonic when she found out she was with child but it didn't work and she blamed herself for his condition."

Dodo stumbled. *What a terrible burden to carry.*

"Lucille thinks his murder could be the gangsters sending her a message by striking at her heart," Dodo said, moving the conversation onto safer ground.

"I wouldn't put nothin' past those mobsters," Beau spat. "Soulless good for nothin's."

"Can't something be done?" asked Rupert.

"When the law is in their pockets, as well as several judges, it makes them untouchable. And if you kick up a fuss, the next thing you know you're in a coffin."

The concept was hard to get her head around and Dodo was thankful that law and order still reigned in England. No wonder Frannie had been so scared.

"Tell me about Tucker Dawson," she said, changing the touchy subject.

"Ah, the competition," conceded Beau. "He seems to be a competent businessman. Owns five clubs uptown and downtown. Definitely cleaner than the way I earn my money." He chuckled. "He's not rotten to the core like Rigatti, but there's something about him I don't trust. Lucille don't wanna sell, and he can't seem to wrap his head around her need for independence."

Side by side, Beau was leagues ahead of Tucker.

"I'm with you about the trust thing," Rupert agreed. "Tucker gets under my skin. Could he want *Lulu's* bad enough to resort to violence?"

"Tucker looks like a thug and he's in bed with Rigatti, sellin' his bootleg stuff at all five of his clubs, but that's more an act of survival—you've seen how Rigatti operates. As much as I don't like the guy, I don't see him as the killer."

"Is there no regulation at all of the illegal alcohol," Rupert asked, as they dodged children playing jacks on the sidewalk with bits of tree bark.

"None, and some batches are lethal, as you can imagine. As for the rest, it's pretty rough. They had to come up with all sorts of new cocktails to cover up the awful flavor."

They crossed over Canal Street and headed for *Lulu's*. She was eating a late lunch out back and called for Kid to feed the new arrivals.

"Is there enough?" asked Rupert.

Lucille barked out a laugh. "That man makes enough food to feed an army. Sit yo'selves down."

"How's Eula Mae?" asked Dodo.

"'Bout as bad as you'd imagine. I told her to take the night off and however many more she needs."

"Is she safe?" asked Rupert. "Can I help?"

Lucille slapped her knee. "Honey, unless you put on a few pounds and carry a large gun, I don't think you're quite what she needs. I sent Tucker."

Rupert paled as Beau's face creased in panic. "Why not send me, Lulu?"

"I'd already sent you on an errand, Beau." Her tone to him was softer than usual.

He took Lulu's hand in his bear claw. "Well, when Tucker needs a break, I'd consider it an honor to provide protection for Eula Mae."

"I'll keep that in mind, sugar."

"Did you by any chance remember to ask Eula Mae about that package?" asked Dodo.

"I did but she didn't know what I was talking about," replied Lucille as she directed Kid where to lay the food.

Then someone removed the package. Why?

"Ah, the English have arrived," said Tucker Dawson in a low voice as they entered the house like backdoor neighbors. "Eula Mae's asleep upstairs," he explained. "Minnie is sitting with Clyde in the parlor. She sent everyone else home." He laid his cigar on a saucer on the still unfinished table.

Dodo knew that the funeral was scheduled for the following day and that someone sat with the body to make sure it did not wake up. She realized for the first time how the term 'wake' had developed.

"It's you we came to talk to," she responded.

"Oh?" An emotion she couldn't analyze clouded Tucker's scarred face and he fiddled with the cigar.

"I'm looking into the—" she dropped her voice "—murder."

Tucker's shoulders shot up. "I didn't have nothin' to do with it!"

Rupert put a hand on the back of his chair and Dodo waved her hands to indicate that Tucker should keep his voice quieter.

"I am not accusing you, Mr. Dawson. I merely need to fill in the background in order to be able to draw some intelligent conclusions."

His shoulders dropped. "Don't know that I'll be much help."

"Are you from New Orleans?" Dodo began.

"Born and raised."

"Uptown or downtown?" She was beginning to understand the geography.

Tucker smirked. "Learning the lingo already, Mizz Dorchester. I like it."

She squirmed. "Seems the least I can do."

"Downtown. But my mother was white, if you must know. Her family disowned her. My pops drove cabs for other men. Never saved enough money to buy his own automobile. Then he died. It was a hard scrabble, but we managed. I even put a bit by. As jazz evolved, I saw an opportunity and sunk my money into a rickety buildin' downtown. A real honky tonk, it was. But I worked hard. Never takin' a vacation. Got five now. My mama sure is proud of me and we both live uptown. We are re-spected."

Dodo did not doubt it. "I understand you have three sons."

Tucker flattened his lips. "That's right. Me and my wife, God rest her soul, had three boys. They help me run the clubs. We're always lookin' to expand which is why I'm hopin' Lulu will sell to me. Then she wouldn't have to deal with the likes of Rigatti no more. She could spend her time making new records."

If that was the way this town was run, Tucker did have a point. It wasn't like Lucille needed the money from the club. Her music had made her wealthy and would continue to do so for years to come.

"How long have you known Lucille and Eula Mae?" she continued.

"We all grew up around the same area downtown. When Lulu started singin' as a child in church, I knew she was goin' places. I invited her to sing at my first club. You could say she got her big break from me." He brushed lint from his sleeve and self-satisfaction rippled across his blunt features. "Lulu learned the uptown ways pretty fast once she and her daddy started makin' it big." He raised his eyes to the ceiling. "Eula Mae not so much." He adjusted his sleeves which winked with diamond studded cufflinks. "Lulu draws plenty of attention with that voice. Ain't no one can compare. And she ain't hard to look at either. Soon as they moved uptown, 'bout fifteen years ago, I booked her for several of my uptown clubs. I was still married then. But we became friends again and when her Daddy and Lonnie started *Lulu's*, I offered some advice. We go *way* back." He glanced at Rupert. "Eula Mae's part of the package."

Dodo pulled out a chair. "So, you knew Clyde well?"

"I remember when Lulu moved Eula Mae and Clyde into this house and gave her the job. He was just a young'un then. Cute little thing. Followed her around like a duckling and fell asleep on a little bed in the kitchen at *Lulu's*. Only natural he'd end up working there."

"Did you ever see him have any kind of trouble at the club?" Dodo asked.

"Clyde was—how do I put it? Above the fray." He ran a hand over his square head. "I'm sure you noticed he was lackin' in some ways. His mother was fiercely protective and if anyone made trouble, she got madder 'an a hornet and let 'em know it. Meant folks left Clyde alone."

Dodo ran a hand over the stain. It was no longer sticky. "What about children at school? They can be mean."

"All I know is he left school in the fifth grade. He'd learned to read a little and do basic math. But I think Eula Mae was worried he'd get bullied when he got older."

"*Was* he bullied?"

Tucker considered. "I don't know. I'm not that close to them. Maybe, you know how kids are."

The theory that Clyde's death was tied to the club was taking up space in Dodo's head. "Has there ever been any trouble at *Lulu's*?"

"Other than from Rigatti? No. Wait! I do think there was some disagreement with the outfit that provides the seafood once. Can't remember the details. You should ask Lulu about it."

Rupert caught her eye.

"You were at *Lulu's* the night Clyde was killed. What time did you arrive?"

"Around nine thirty. Before that, I was in a showdown with one of Rigatti's goons. You can check if you like."

He gave her the name.

Chapter 11

"What do you think?" Rupert asked Dodo as they left Tucker at Eula Mae's.

"Personally, I still think he's a shifty character and I'm not sure I believe anything he says. He's a world-class bootlicker, like a perfectly good apple that hides a worm. I'd like to check out his alibi. If the murder happened between eight and ten, he certainly had time to commit the deed and be at *Lulu's* by nine-thirty."

"I believe Tucker's offer to check his alibi was a bluff. It might ruffle his feathers and reveal the rot beneath," said Rupert, concern lacing his comment.

"True. Perhaps we can send the burly Beau."

"I like that plan better," he pronounced. "Our presence anywhere is rather conspicuous."

"Agreed."

The distance between Eula Mae's and *Lulu's* was so short, they were already back, their reflections looking back at Dodo from the club window. "I'd like to question Kid. He saw Clyde day to day and would have noticed any changes in his behavior or disposition. He might have insights no one else does."

Like old hands, they walked round to the back of *Lulu's* and straight into the kitchen where the air was heavy with the distinctive Cajun spices. It was little more than a fancy hut, about fourteen by fourteen feet. In the very middle was an enormous prep table that was currently full of eye-watering onions. Kid was chopping them with a practiced hand at lightning speed. Windows on three sides maximized the Louisiana sunshine. An enormous black iron oven, boasting eight stove tops, sat against the wall without windows. Large black pots sung like drunken grandmas as their contents bubbled and boiled, their lids failing to keep the scalding liquids at bay.

"Howdy," said Kid, pausing from his labors. "What can I do for you folks? Hungry?"

"No, no!" Dodo assured him. "I was wondering if you'd have time for a word?"

Kid's features descended into confusion.

"A chat," Rupert explained.

"Oh." He looked around at the pile of vibrantly colored ingredients and shrugged. "I guess five minutes wouldn't hurt." He motioned with the knife and met Dodo and Rupert at one of the outdoor tables with a full glass of iced tea.

"Do you have a real name?" began Dodo.

Kid grinned, showing the gap in his teeth. "My mama named me Cuthbert William Calhoun, but my papa never took to it and called me Kid before I could talk."

"Have you worked here a long time?" Dodo asked, watching him take a long swig from the sugary nectar like a man rescued from a desert.

"Since the day old Mr. Bassett opened the joint." Kid spoke with such a heavy southern accent that Dodo had to listen especially hard to understand.

"Do you mind if I ask how you got the job?"

Snapping his wrinkled fingers he replied, "We was neighbors, downtown. My mama was the best cook in the whole of Lou'siana. She taught me everythin' she knew. Mr. Bassett took me on for a trial run and I'm still here today. Good pay, good hours, good company."

"Your mama must have been an amazing cook," said Rupert.

Kid nodded, eyes down, hand worrying the cauliflower ear. "She was."

"I suppose you knew Clyde as well as anyone, what with him hanging out in here as a child while Eula Mae worked and then working here himself?"

Kid tipped his head and winked, like a pirate. "I seen him more'n my own grandchildren."

"How many do you have?" she asked.

"Thirty-five," he said with a cracked grin.

"My goodness!" responded Dodo. "How many children do you have?"

"Eight living. Two in the ground."

Dodo blinked. "And you still live downtown?"

"Decatur and Toulouse," he said with a nod. "Same house I's born in. But with the wages Mizz Lulu pays me, we was able to buy the house next door, too. Knocked the walls down myself." He finished the tea and wiped his mouth with the back of his hand. "My pappy was a freed slave 'afore the civil war. My momma too. But he gone and got hisself killed in that there war, leaving my mama with six mouths to feed. Started cookin' and sellin' her food right out of that old house to make ends meet. We all pitched in. My mother's rep'etation grew and grew till she was known in all of New Orleens. Even the rich, white, and Creole ladies would order her food. Whole city mourned when my momma died."

Though Dodo was fascinated by Kid's personal history, she was well aware that time was short and he'd have to get back to the kitchen soon. "What was Clyde like? Did he have any friends."

Kid's lips formed a furrowed circle. "I'm sure it's no secret he was…limited." He touched his own head. "Makes it hard to find real friends and Eula Mae was fierce 'bout protectin' him. She was his best friend. Mizz Lulu, a close second." He wiped the corner of his eye with his stained apron. "I'd like to think he counted me as one."

"Eula Mae mentioned a man by the name of Bubba Swanson who gave him some trouble when they were young."

Kid's chin dropped as his brows rose. "Not since that half-baked biscuit fell out of a tree a week ago! Broke both legs."

At least she could scratch Bubba off her list.

"Was Clyde good at his job? Did he ever want to cook?"

Features pinched with indignation, Kid retorted, "I wouldn't let that chil' *near* a sharp knife. Chop his fingers off, fo' sure. But he was a good waiter once he learned to balance them there dishes." Kid chuckled. "At the beginnin' he dropped more'n a few. Sent Eula Mae howlin' after him. But he got it in the end."

Dodo had a burst of inspiration. "Did he have any secrets he kept from Eula Mae?"

Narrowing his eyes, Kid murmured, "Wouldn't want to get the chil' in no trouble."

"He's out of the reach of trouble now," Rupert remarked.

"I don't want to blacken his rep'etation, none."

Dodo's senses piqued.

"If I'm going to find his killer, I need to know everything I can." She crept forward on her chair. "So, Clyde had secrets?"

A rush of air passed Kid's dry lips. "His mama never knew, but he used to go down to the port to watch the ships and boats. Drawn to 'em like ants to sugar pie. Eula Mae didn't like him goin' near the river 'cos he couldn't swim." He ran a rough finger stained with spices across his lip. "She thought he was safe at 'ome, but most times he was boat watchin'."

Not exactly the scandalous skeleton Dodo had been expecting.

"Do you think something may have happened at the port that led to his death?"

Kid stared off into space. "'Bout a month ago, he came back, cheeks all bright, eyes kind 'a wild. Thought p'rhaps he had a scare but when I pushed, he wouldn't tell me nothin'."

"Did Eula Mae notice?" Dodo asked, her heart kicking up a notch.

"We was busier than a church fan in dog days that night for a weddin' party. No time to notice." He looked up from his empty glass. "Do y'all think I's wrong not to push him? That it was somethin' dangerous?"

"If he wouldn't tell you, don't blame yourself," said Dodo. "But it does give me a new line of inquiry."

The face accustomed to hard work did not appear convinced of his innocence in the matter.

"You've been very helpful," Dodo assured him.

Turning to make his way back to the kitchen, he teared up.

"Well, that's something of interest," Rupert said as they watched Kid amble over to the kitchen door. "I suppose that means we're headed to the port."

As they jumped onto a streetcar, Rupert asked, "What're your plans when we get there? See how the land lies? Nose around?"

Dodo looked out the window. "I suppose so. But we'll have to be careful not to tip anyone off. We must look like ordinary tourists. I'm hoping for a spark of inspiration once we get there."

The tram let them out at the bustling port and they wandered along docks full of muscular stevedores swinging loads off barges and onto the wharf. The workers eyed them both suspiciously. Seeing nothing overtly untoward and spotting a coffee shop, Dodo suggested they stop for a drink. "Places like that are a haven for local gossip."

A redheaded, freckled, young woman approached their table, and after they had ordered, she dropped her voice and declared, "I love your dress, miss. You don't see things like that in New Orleens. Are y'all from New York?"

Dodo had to smother a snort. "Thank you. Actually, we're from across the pond."

"Lake Pontchartrain?"

"The Atlantic. We're from England," explained Rupert.

The waitress's cheeks flushed red and her mossy eyes twinkled with excitement. "Oh, my heck! Y'all are not! I never met an English person before!"

Eager to exploit the girl's interest, Dodo asked, "I say, do you know much about the docks?"

"Oh, yes, miss. Lived here my whole life."

"We were wondering about the place." Dodo decided to get right to the point. "Are there any problems with smuggling? It's a huge issue in London."

The girl looked over her shoulder. "I'd say every port in the world has problems of the sort, wouldn't you?"

Rupert's brow hiked up with curiosity. "What kinds of products are smuggled? Whiskey?"

"No sir, not since Prohibition. More like tobacco and cocaine."

"And this goes on under the officials' noses?" Dodo asked.

The waitress checked the whereabouts of the manager then bent down to whisper, "Well, a bribe goes a long way 'round here, or so I hear."

"A young friend of ours used to spend a lot of time watching the boats by the water," Dodo continued.

"Lots of people pass the time that way," the waitress agreed turning to leave.

"Our friend's name was Clyde—"

The girl spun around, her amber curls bouncing. "Oh! I *know* him!"

Dodo couldn't believe her luck. "We're worried he may have been muddled up in something like smuggling."

"Really? He doesn't seem the type. I see Clyde on my way home from work, sometimes. He's a shy boy and I'm not supposed to speak to him because—well, you know, but he asks me questions and it would be rude not to answer, I say. But now that you mention it, I haven't seen him the last couple of days." She looked around as if he might walk past the restaurant.

Dodo's stomach plummeted. "Then I'm sorry to have to tell you that he was killed."

The girl slapped a hand to her mouth. "No!" Her big green eyes flashed over her fingers. "Do you know why? Was it the smugglers?"

"We don't know. I was hoping someone here at the port might know something—"

"Miss Boothe!" cried a buxom lady who was obviously the coffee shop manager. "Quit your lollygagging, girl!"

The waitress snapped to attention. "I'll have to go fetch your coffee, but when I come back there's something I simply *must* tell you." She whirled on her heel and hurried away.

"How fortuitous!" declared Rupert. "What do you think she knows?"

"Kid said Clyde came back a couple of weeks ago all flustered. I'm hoping she knows something about that mystery."

Dodo began drumming the table with her fingers until she saw the girl weaving her way back through the tables holding a tray.

Miss Boothe placed the cups on the table and pretended to move the coffee pot and cups around to give herself more time. Flashing her eyes up to check on the whereabouts of her boss, she whispered, "Y'all, Clyde was anxious one day when I was goin' home for lunch. I asked him what was wrong, and he told me he saw someone crawl out of the bottom of a boat, climb up the riverbank and slink away, but not before lockin' eyes with Clyde and glarin' at him something fierce. Clyde was all shook up."

"A stowaway?" asked Rupert. "I'm sure that happens a lot."

"Yes, but this one had blood all over his face."

Chapter 12

"Blood?" responded Dodo trying to keep her voice down.

"Clyde was sweating bullets. So, I said the first thing that came into my head to calm him down. I said, perhaps he's a butcher."

"Did it work?"

"Clyde was innocent, like a child. It seemed to, but I really believe it was a bad person. I kept my wits about me for a while after that."

"Did Clyde describe the man in any other way?"

"Not really, except to say that he rocked when he walked."

The lady manager reappeared and Miss Boothe glanced in her direction with a knitted brow.

"Thank you, Miss Boothe," said Dodo.

"Oh, call me Nellie." The manager was now giving her the evil eye, and Nellie moved to a table that had just been taken by a mother and her child.

"People with a limp might be described as walking with a rocking motion," said Rupert. "Or someone with a peg leg." He smirked.

"A bloody-faced pirate," said Dodo withdrawing a notebook from her bag with a grin. "Though that's right up your alley, I say we're getting a little fanciful." She opened up the pad. "Now, I have a whole litany of suspects, including the bloody pirate, that I need to organize on paper." She fished out a pencil. "Right. Who's first?"

"I think Rigatti has to be at the top of the list," said Rupert. "But I don't want it to be him since he's apparently above the law and Clyde won't get any justice. Plus, accusations in that direction will just lead to more deaths."

Dodo wrote *Rigatti* at the top.

"His motive is strong since Lucille hasn't caved to his demands."

"As for opportunity, he has any number of bag men who could do the dastardly deed for him," said Rupert. "That makes him the prime suspect."

"Hold on! I see a problem. Remember the evidence at the scene indicated that Clyde knew the killer. They either let themselves in and he stayed sitting at the table, or he went to the back door to let them in—suggested by the smudge of stain on the frame by the back door—and felt comfortable enough to sit back at the table and resume his work."

Rupert shrugged. "Rigatti's tentacles spread far. He could have some of Lucille's workers on his payroll. Remember what Frannie said. They wouldn't raise an alarm with Clyde."

She pointed her pencil at him. "An astute observation, Mr. Danforth, and not one to ignore. Though I hate to think of any of Lucille's friends as a traitor."

She scribbled the information in the notebook while Rupert drank his coffee.

"Next, the nocturnal window washer. Everything about that is suspicious. Were they looking for the illusive package or were they trying to see if Clyde was alone?"

"Put Tucker on the list too," said Rupert.

"You suspect him?"

"As I've mentioned before, that chap rubs me the wrong way. I think he bears investigating more. *And* he wants to buy *Lulu's*. If Lucille is shaken by Clyde's death, her vulnerability might make it easier to negotiate with her."

"Agreed." She wrote it all down. "I'm putting Auggie on the list too. I have no idea of his motive, but he certainly plays a part in this game and is someone Clyde would recognize."

She placed her elbows on the table.

"You forgot about the pirate." Rupert screwed up one eye, hitching up the side of his mouth and making her laugh out loud until the stares from the other patrons reminded her where she was.

"You're not going to list Beau or Kid?" Rupert asked.

Her eyes came up from the book to meet his gaze. "I know I usually suspect everyone but Beau is such a gentle giant, and though she claims otherwise, Lucille trusts him. She might even love him."

"What about Kid?"

"Would he have had the time?" she asked.

"We've seen him take a break to talk with us. By the evening, all the preparation has been done. He could say he had a call of nature and hurry round to Eula Mae's. It's not far," suggested Rupert.

"How old do you think he is?"

"It's hard to tell. He's rather grizzled and stoops as he works. Sixty? Sixty-five?" replied Rupert balancing the coffee spoon on his finger. "But he's energetic for his age."

"I agree, it's not impossible. But what's his motive?"

"You always say money is the usual motive."

"True. Perhaps we can poke about a bit. I'll put them on the list." She tapped the pencil on the pad. "Going back to your pirate. Nellie said Clyde was terrified of him. If that's the case, he would not have let the pirate into the house without a struggle and he would probably have yelled out in fear. There was no sign of a skirmish and Miss Frannie didn't hear anything. Though, I grant you, an evil looking stranger is a preferable villain, but I don't think it fits the facts as they stand."

"What about the neighbors, Mizz Minnie and Mizz Frannie?" Rupert tried to mimic their southern accent and Dodo burst out laughing again.

"Mimicry is not your specialty, darling. Nor mine. Can you really see the tiny Miss Minnie having the strength to strangle anyone? And remember, the bruises on his neck were wide, indicating a man's fingers."

"This is why *you* are the detective." He smiled and she got lost in it for a moment.

"Then there's the bombing. It happened so close to Clyde's death that it makes me wonder if they are connected in any way."

"Could that be why someone wrote 'rat' on the door?" asked Rupert. "Could Clyde have seen something and it was a warning not to inform on someone?"

"Fat lot of good that would do him in this town anyway. But it is a possibility, I suppose."

She placed the pencil and notepad back in her bag, drank the rest of the coffee, and stood. Once outside, they wandered back to the tram stop as birds circled overhead.

"It feels much better to have everything down on paper, but I need time to let it all stew," she said. "Fancy a trip to *Lafitte's* blacksmith's shop?"

Lafitte's was a small, white plaster building whose front was made up of three sets of wooden double doors on the front and one set on the side with a window on each end. A sign out the front told them it was built in 1722 in the Briquette-Entre-Poteauxe, or brick between posts, method of construction, used at that time in Louisiana. The building was used by the Lafitte brothers, Jean and Pierre as a base for their smuggling operation.

The only remnants of the blacksmith's trade were a tall brick fireplace and iron knickknacks on the walls. The place had been a bar for the better part of fifty years, but since Prohibition, it had become an eatery serving muffalettas and cola during the day. She suspected they sold the hard stuff at night. The thick walls provided cool relief from the heat outside and they each ordered the Louisiana sandwich and a cola.

Dodo could almost feel the ghosts of the past in the atmospheric room. Behind the scarred wooden bar was a rough wall with shelves holding cups and plates. A door intersected the wall hiding the kitchen from the patrons.

When the waiter returned with their items, he laid a bill next to Rupert's plate and gave a quick salute.

"Good gracious! This is amazing!" cried Dodo as she chewed the first bite of the fresh, fragrant bread, stuffed with ham and olive salad.

As they sat, enjoying the food and the respite from the sun, Auggie Benoit appeared behind the bar.

"Hello!" said Dodo in surprise.

"Hello!" Auggie responded. "*Mais là*! Didn't you know I own this place? It's no jazz club but the tourists like it. How's the food?"

"Delicious," Dodo replied. "I'm wondering how I can recreate it in England."

"Well, my version is a secret family recipe." He tapped the side of his nose. "It's more than my life's worth to let you in on it."

If Beau had said those same words, it would not have sounded so rude. She had forgotten what an unfriendly demeanor Auggie possessed. How did such a personality succeed in the tourist industry?

"Now, if you'll excuse me. *Au revoir*." He bowed and disappeared again.

"What a thorny fellow. I'm surprised Lucille didn't mention that Auggie was the proprietor," remarked Rupert before taking another bite.

They finished their meal and Dodo checked the time. "We should get back to see if we can help with the preparations for the funeral."

Rupert retrieved some money from his wallet, left it on the table, and swiped the receipt into his pocket.

"Let's go."

Chapter 13

The funeral procession was like nothing Dodo had *ever* experienced.

The ladies of the Benevolent Society had arrived at Eula Mae's early to prepare Clyde for burial. Working together they formed an efficient, kind band of sisters who sought to bring comfort to the bereaved by removing all the stresses of preparing a funeral. The ladies were all dressed alike—a simple uniform with white shirtwaists, black skirts, black hats, and gloves. Each also wore a silver sash.

The kitchen table groaned under the weight of food for the luncheon. Eula Mae's friends and neighbors had rallied around in her time of need. Dodo nodded to Miss Frannie and Miss Minnie as they brought in their contribution. The whole house was filled with a spirit of solace and compassion.

The English visitors had been invited to walk in the second line of the procession and had been given black and silver armbands to wear on their mourning clothes. This placed them after the family, close friends, and the brass band. Members of the band also wore a uniform, but theirs consisted of black jackets, white shirts, black hats, black and white shoes, and the silver sash. The visual effect was dramatic, but the acoustic effect was even more emotional as they played the sweet strains of *Amazing Grace* from deep within their souls all the way to the church.

A horse drawn hearse led the procession as Eula Mae, held up by Lucille, walked behind with other close friends. The tragic convoy snaked through the colorful streets as people stopped on the sidewalks out of respect, hats to hearts.

The Louisiana sun shone with full strength in a cloudless sky, the burning heat absorbing into Dodo's dark mourning clothes. Beads of sweat formed all over her body, trickling down her back and temples. She hoped the church wasn't too far away for fear of fainting. She glanced at Lizzie who was wiping her face with a handkerchief.

The little Baptist church was far too small for the number of mourners. Bursting at the seams, people stood around the edges and in the aisles. The preacher, who Dodo had learned from Lucille was the same man who had christened Clyde as a baby and counseled Eula Mae through the whole ordeal of her pregnancy, gave a tender, heartfelt eulogy, reading comforting scriptures about resurrection from the New Testament. Coupled with the impassioned choir, Dodo's heart was truly stirred.

Once outside, beside the burial plot, Dodo noticed that all the graves were *above* ground. Poor Eula Mae was inconsolable as she gazed on the casket.

The band and procession reconvened and weaved their way back to Eula Mae's modest home, this time playing jollier music in celebration of Clyde's life. It was a tremendous and inspirational send off for a blameless boy who had died too young.

At Eula Mae's house, Dodo and company found only standing room, but in spite of the crush, the place suffered from the vacuum that all houses of mourning exhibit. A beloved light had been extinguished that nothing could replace. Friends consoled friends in quiet tones and low conversations.

In addition to the spread put on by the ladies of the Benevolent Society, Kid had pulled out all the stops with heaping piles of steaming crawdads and oysters.

The English contingent remained in a corner of the hall, holding their plates tightly while surveying the grieving crowd.

"I wonder why they don't bury the dead in the ground?" mused Dodo.

"Oh," began Ernie. "I asked someone at the cemetery and they explained that it's because New Orleans is below sea level. It means the water table is very high, and you hit water long before you reach six feet. If they buried the coffin in the watery soil, it would become waterlogged and even dislodge."

"Ah, that makes perfect sense," responded Dodo.

"What did you think of the jazzy musical parade?" asked Rupert digging into a white pudding.

"I rather liked it," Dodo replied. "The intense fervor of the hymns was exceptionally moving. Less formal than we're used to, of course. I know in some cases in England we do have the family follow the hearse, but it's all very silent with only the somber bells tolling. Gut wrenching, actually. However, I don't think this sort of thing would catch on at home. We're much too stiff and rigid."

"I agree," responded Rupert.

She spotted workers from the club in groups of two and three talking in hushed tones. Tucker Dawson and Auggie Benoit were also in attendance, looking uncomfortable and out of place at the other end of the hall.

A sharp knock at the front door was hardly audible above the low chatter. Beau opened it to reveal Rigatti. Stoney faced, Beau asked, "What're you doing here, Pat? You know you're not welcome. I'll let Mizz Eula Mae know you came by to offer your condolences. Now be on your way, we've got enough trouble."

"You need to improve your manners, Buckley," growled the mobster. "My well wishes are as valuable as anyone else's. Now, you'd better let me in."

Beau's massive frame blocked the door. "Ain't happening, pal."

Man to man, Rigatti was no match for Beau and the two men stood baring teeth like two wild dogs.

Dodo's heart sank as Eula Mae stepped out of the parlor. "What's this?"

"Pat was just leaving," explained Beau.

When Eula Mae saw who it was, all the heartache, all the sorrow, all the wondering who could have harmed her boy rose to the top of her soul like sugar reaching boiling point.

"Get out!" she screamed. "Get out! Isn't it enough to know y'all killed my boy without coming to twist the knife." She raised her arms as if she were about to assault Rigatti, who didn't flinch, though his hostile expression brimmed with malice. Beau grabbed Eula Mae, wrapping his arms around hers, pulling her against him as she struggled like a catfish on a line.

"Go on home, Pat. You've made your point."

Rigatti scowled and touched his hat in a counterfeit act of manners. "You go slandering my name like that and I'll make trouble for you, Eula Mae. I had nothin' to do with your boy's death and I'm insulted you would think I did. You'd better watch your mouth."

Beau locked eyes with Eula Mae and slightly shook his head. Rigatti strutted away, shoulders stiff and straight, as tears streamed down Eula Mae's anguished face.

Lucille pushed her way into the hall and taking one look at her friend, took Eula Mae in her own arms whispering to her like a mother to a baby.

That evening, Rupert and Dodo sat out on Lucille's porch, recovering from the emotional exhaustion of the day and watching sweethearts walk by. Lucille was staying with Eula Mae and had taken over a sleeping draught. A gentle, evening breeze stirred the hanging moss on the large oak trees and the distant strains of jazz created a soothing soundtrack for the pensive mood.

"How's the investigation coming along, m'lady?" asked Lizzie, holding hands with her fiancée, Ernie, in a daring demonstration of public affection. "Eula Mae seems to think it was that gangster, Rigatti. Do you agree?"

"With his violent reputation I cannot possibly leave him off my list," Dodo replied. "Especially since he and his goons seem to kill indiscriminately without fear of indictment. But his vehement denial has stayed with me. His sort would proudly claim responsibility, if you ask me. Yet he didn't."

"Lizzie and I went to visit the cathedral yesterday," said Ernie. "While we were there, we met some other people in service, and we started chatting. We got around to the murder, of course, and they were of the opinion that it *wasn't* Rigatti this time. As you have concluded, m'lady, they believed he would strut around town letting everyone know it was him as a warning to others. They also informed us that the rumor mill is saying that Rigatti was not responsible for that bombing, either."

Dodo sat forward. "Really?"

"Yes," chimed in Lizzie. "Apparently, some of his thugs are confused as they know it wasn't them. They're worried another gang is trying to take over their turf."

Dodo's mind started to grind. If Rigatti wasn't behind the bombing, who was? How did that fact change her preconceptions? Did it alter her own theorizing about Clyde's murder?

"You asked how my investigation was coming along," she finally responded, her thoughts darting in all directions. "By this point, I usually have it narrowed down to a couple of people of interest but not this time. In this place, with its underbelly of violence, there are just too many suspects. Without even considering the suspicious outsiders who keep popping up. It's very messy." She looked up feeling exasperated. "I have to confess, I'm at a loss."

"Suspicious strangers?" asked Ernie.

"Clyde crossed paths with a mysterious stowaway covered in blood?" explained Rupert.

Dodo recounted to Ernie and Lizzie what the waitress at the coffee shop had told them. "But at this juncture, that's all he is—a mysterious, menacing figure. There's nothing to link him to Clyde's death other than a fleeting interaction."

An aromatic pile of beignets sat in a bowl on the table but no one moved to take one.

"Then there's the shadowy window washer," added Rupert.

"He's even more elusive than the stowaway," remarked Dodo. "We have no idea who he is. All we have to go on is a poor description from the neighbor and the fact that it's unusual to wash windows at dusk."

"That and the neighbor telling us that Clyde washes their windows. So, Eula Mae wouldn't have paid someone else to do them," clarified Rupert. "And then there's the misdelivered package that never made it to Eula Mae's, or it did but was removed before she ever saw it."

"I see what you mean, m'lady," agreed Lizzie. "Too many loose ends and not enough solid evidence."

"Exactly." Dodo stirred her cola with a straw. "The only thing I'm sure about is that the killer was a man because of the size of the bruises on Clyde's neck."

The hair on the back of Dodo's neck stood on end. *Was someone watching her?* She looked around while the others called out theories, but spotting no one, she rejoined the conversation.

"What I need is an eyewitness or a really good clue," she said. "But my main problem is that I can see no motive to kill the poor boy."

After a moment of reflection, Ernie steered them in a completely different direction by relating what he had learned about the area in his meeting with the knowledgeable lady historian.

"I'm going up to prepare your bedroom, m'lady," said Lizzie, after Ernie had finished his report.

Ernie checked his watch. "I should do the same, sir."

100

"I'll come up as well," said Dodo. "I really want a bath to wash off all the sadness of the day." She kissed Rupert on the tip of his nose and followed her maid into the house.

Lucille only had one bathroom on the upper floor, but it was fabulously luxurious. Lizzie drew the bath, filling it with lavender scented salts. Dodo slid beneath the water, holding her breath, listening to the odd, muted sounds of the house.

When she resurfaced, she tried to gather her unruly thoughts concerning Clyde's murder. What event had occurred that had led to Clyde's death? Remembering the ugly graffiti on their front door confirmed that Clyde had witnessed something and was killed to keep him quiet. But what? The bombing?

Once the hot water had cooled, her smooth, young skin prune like, she stepped into a plush robe, wrapping her short, ebony hair in a thick towel. Having instructed Lizzie to go to bed, she returned to her room, removed the towel and brushed her wet hair. It would have to air dry. Lizzie would style it in the morning.

The wood floor creaked as she walked across her room to the open French windows. She breathed in the heady smell of jasmine. Finding the ache of sorrow exhausting, she flopped onto the bed, hair still wet, and promptly fell asleep.

Clyde was calling out to her, his arms outstretched, their fingers almost meeting, but she could not reach him. He began banging on her door.

"M'lady," called a man's voice that was not Clyde's. The knocking continued. "M'lady!"

The thumping finally broke through her dream and she realized it was the voice of Rupert's valet, Ernest.

"Yes?" she cried, gathering her wits.

"It's Mr. Danforth, m'lady. He appears to have been kidnapped!"

Chapter 14

Had Dodo heard wrong?

Heart thudding, while her stomach cramped with fright, she hurried to the bedroom door. Ernie stood, wild-eyed, lines of strain rippling around his young eyes. She dropped her gaze to his hand which held a piece of paper. He offered it to her.

> *Stop yor snoopin' or y'all neva see yor boyfrend agin. Stop pokin yor Inglish noz were it don't belong. Stop or else!*

She raised worried eyes to Ernie's. "Where did you find this?"

"On the porch table. The kidnappers must have been hiding, then attacked him when the rest of us went to bed."

Dodo recalled the feeling she'd experienced that they were being watched.

Hand to her head, her insides lurched. *How could this be happening?* The handwriting was little more than chicken scratch, the spelling, atrocious. She lifted the crumpled note to her nose. *Spices.* What use was a clue like that? In this town, those seasonings were everywhere.

"What do you want to do, m'lady?"

Lizzie appeared behind her fiancé. "What's going on?"

"Someone has kidnapped Mr. Danforth!"

"No!" Lizzie braced herself against the wall and looked about her as if the danger were still present. "When?"

"Last night. After we went to bed. Mr. Danforth said he would undress himself," Ernie responded as Dodo was still recoiling from the devastating news. "What shall we do?"

Dodo placed a palm to her clammy forehead. "Clearly, we cannot apply to the corrupt police. The note implies that I am close to finding the murderer but *I* feel like I've made no progress in my investigation into the death of Clyde at all."

"If you will excuse me for contradicting you, m'lady," began Ernie in an apologetic tone. "But that must not be accurate. Someone is obviously worried that you are getting close to unveiling them."

"But who?" asked Dodo a rising panic threatening to overwhelm her and wishing they had never come to America at all. Rupert could be dead. *Dead!* She would never be able to marry him now. It was too late.

Pull yourself together, girl! The only way you can help Rupert is to maintain a clear head.

"My first thought is Rigatti," she said, finally getting control of her fears. "He seems to be the mastermind of all the crime around here."

"I'm sorry, but how on earth do you expect to confront him?" asked Ernie. "And would it even be wise? He might shoot us on the spot!"

"I *have* to meet him, Ernie."

"I just don't know if that will be possible, m'lady. He has a cadre of bodyguards."

Dodo had an idea. "I'll appeal to Lucille. She'll know how to arrange a meeting." Addressing Lizzie she said, "Help me get dressed and ready. I need to go to Eula Mae's immediately."

"What?" cried Lucille through gritted teeth.

"Rupert has been kidnapped! I need you to set up a meeting with Patrick Rigatti."

Lucille just about choked. "What in Sam Hill? That's one of the craziest ideas I ever heard!"

"Can you suggest a better strategy?" retorted Dodo whose fragile emotions had hardened into steely determination.

"Well...I..." Lucille finally shook her head. "No."

"Alright then. Lizzie and Ernie can stay with Eula Mae—"

"With respect, m'lady. I'm coming with you. Mr. Danforth is *my* employer," declared Ernie. "And he would expect me to protect you in his absence."

"Alright. Let's go!" Dodo compromised, agreeing that having a man with them was probably wise. She headed for the door as Lucille pulled a light wrap around her shoulders.

They hailed a taxi and Lucille directed the driver to Rigatti's headquarters on Franklin Street. Dodo looked up at a conservative building, bookended by two similar buildings. No one would suspect that a master criminal operated out of there.

Walking inside, a pretty, young receptionist looked up in surprise. "Can I help you?"

"We're here to see Rigatti," demanded Lucille.

"Do you have an appointment? *Mr.* Rigatti only sees people by appointment."

"He'll see me," sneered Lulu. "Tell him Lucille Bassett is here."

Dragging her gaze from Dodo, the receptionist looked at Lucille and recognition dawned. "One moment."

She picked up the telephone and punched a button. "There's a Mizz Bassett here to see you, sir."

All they could hear was squawking. The receptionist replaced the receiver, her face contorted with pity.

"He'll see you. Level four." She pointed to the elevator.

Dodo's insides were a fury of emotion and she tried to think of what to say as they rattled up to the fourth floor.

"Now don't you go shooting your mouth off before your brain is loaded. Let me do the talkin'," said Lucille firmly.

"But I—" began Dodo.

Lucille held up a hand. "Uh-uh. Let me."

The elevator faced a door guarded by two men in suits who nodded.

Lucille opened the door and they all filed into a lavishly decorated room that redefined luxury, if not taste. European works of art, which Dodo suspected were originals, lined the walls.

In the middle of the room sat a grotesque, oak desk and sitting behind it, trying to look like a legitimate businessman, was Patrick Rigatti.

Forming a pyramid with his chubby hands, the squirrely tyrant glared at them with his good eye, like a lion sizing up his next meal.

With features hard as nails he whined, "To what do I owe this pleasure, Mizz Bassett. Ready to sell?"

Lucille straightened her shoulders. "I'm here on other business, Rigatti."

The gangster's mean eyes narrowed. "I'm not getting' your meanin', Mizz Bassett."

Dodo whipped out the note and Lucille placed it on his desk. He glanced at the wrinkled paper then lifted a furrowed brow. "And you think *I* left this?"

"Didn't you?" Lucille barked.

He laughed. A throaty, vulgar sound. "No, I did not. In case you hadn't noticed, I'm not that subtle. I'd a' killed him where he sat."

"I don't believe you," said Lucille in a level tone.

"Well, I certainly can't control what you do and don't believe, Mizz Bassett, but I don't even know who this fella is." He nodded toward Dodo. "Your boyfriend, I take it." Leering, he continued, "Though if the situation is vacant, I wouldn't mind applying." He winked.

Dodo's stomach twisted with disgust.

"So, you're denying that you kidnapped Rupert Danforth," Lucille snapped.

"Who?" He leaned back in his blood red, leather chair, surveying them. "Oh, the boyfriend. What possible interest would I have in kidnappin' him?" His tone had turned dangerous.

"Because you killed Eula Mae's boy and want to stop Mizz Dorchester here uncoverin' the fact."

105

The expression on his square, stubbled face might be described as a smile, but it bore no humor. "Well, that would be very clever of her because I didn't do it."

The pair were locked in a precarious standoff. Dodo didn't doubt there was a loaded gun in his desk.

"You are denyin' the murder and the kidnappin'," Lucille tried again.

Rigatti placed a stubby hand over his heart. "I most certainly am! You better believe if I'd done those things, I would not do them in secret. Part of my...clout is achieved by taking credit for my crimes. When people know that I am responsible, it fosters respect."

"Is that why you bombed the *Hurdy Gurdy?*" Lucille was coming to a boil.

Ernest stepped forward, which action earned a snort of contempt from Rigatti.

He stroked the scars around his eye. "Who said it was me?"

"Everyone!" declared Lucille.

"Then you make my case for me, Lulu. I don't even have to commit a crime in this town to be held responsible. That only increases my hold over the fine people of New Orleens."

Dodo noticed a minute slump in Lucille's shoulders. She could see Lucille losing faith in their cause before her very eyes. The poison of hysteria began creeping along Dodo's bloodstream again. If Rigatti really wasn't responsible for the bombing, she could see no connection between him, Clyde and Rupert. Her vision blurred and she grabbed onto the back of one of the heavy, claw-footed chairs in front of Rigatti's ridiculous desk. Ernie reached out to steady her.

They were back at square one and time was running out.

"Do you know who *did* set the bomb at the *Hurdy?*" Lucille finally asked after an awkwardly long silence where Rigatti stared at them over ringed fingers.

106

"I do not. But I'd like to thank them. It has saved me the bother. Now the land will lose its value and I'll be able to snap up the property, cheap. Maybe open my *own* club."

Lucille's voice dripped with contempt. "And who would play for a lout like you?"

His good eye sharpened, enjoying the game of cat and mouse. "You'd be surprised."

Lucille took a shaky step back. "I bet I wouldn't."

He pushed his upper lip under his nose. "How closely did you vet that new pianist of yours?"

Dodo jerked her eyes to Lucille.

"I don't believe you."

"Have it your own way. Now, if that is all, I'm a busy man." The danger in his voice ebbed away, replaced by impatience, tired of the game.

Ernie bristled beside her.

As they walked onto the street, trams and cars whizzed by. *How could the world keep turning when her heart was torn to shreds?* Detached from reality, Dodo sensed despair waiting in the wings. Life was going on around her as if Rupert were not in mortal danger. Her breaths became short and shallow, her brain fuzzy.

Lucille blew air through her nose. "Grinnin' like a dead possum! Uggh! I hate that man! And I was sure it was him."

"What can we do now?" Dodo asked, her voice weak and thin.

Lucille grabbed her by the arms. "Don't fall apart on me! Let's use that brain 'a yours. If we take Rigatti off the table, who do we have left?"

Taking an unsteady breath, Dodo gathered her tattered wits and sent despair packing. "The mysterious, nocturnal window washer, a package that was misdelivered that has now disappeared, and an eerie stowaway."

"That ain't much."

"No." Despair poked his nose back onto the stage.

A tram passed and Dodo's glazed eyes connected with a man staring out of the window. A large bloodstain marred his face.

"The menacing stowaway!" Dodo cried, pointing at the tram.

"Taxi!" cried Ernie.

"Follow that tram," demanded Dodo as she and Lucille crushed into the back while Ernie jumped into the passenger seat.

Please don't let Rupert be hurt. Please don't let Rupert be hurt.

The cab followed the tram for four stops before the 'stowaway' jumped off. Dodo hurtled out of the car leaving the others to pay the fare and hurried through the street behind the oddly loping man. As he turned the corner into an alley, she grabbed him by the shoulder.

Startled, he lifted large, rough fists ready to fight. Dodo's eyes were glued to his face where a huge, raspberry birth mark colored one half. *Not blood. Not blood.* She dropped her hands and he followed suit.

"What do you want?" His French accent was strong, his voice rough like he swallowed sandpaper for lunch.

"Did you arrive a few weeks ago as a stowaway?" Dodo asked.

His big, chestnut eyes darted around the street. "Am I in trouble?"

Pulse pounding in her ears she said, "That depends. Have you killed anyone?"

The man took a step back raising both his hands. "Non!"

Ernie and Lucille arrived, gasping.

"What are you doing in New Orleans?" Dodo demanded.

His eyes shifted to the side. "I'm 'ere to find work with my brother. I could not afford ze ship's passage so I 'id in the 'old. I come from Lafourche."

"Have you ever met a man named Clyde?"

His face creased in confusion. "I do not really know anyone 'ere."

Hope was slipping through her fingers like grains of sand.

"Sorry to have bothered you," Ernie said.

The man limped away.

"Looks like Clyde got the wrong end of the stick," said Ernie.

'Yes," sighed Lucille. "Let's go home."

What Dodo really wanted to do was curl up in a ball and wish it all away but that would not bring Rupert back. He needed her. What would she normally do? *Return to the scene of the crime.*

As they arrived back at the house she walked up to the porch and examined the table carefully with her eyes and hands. Squatting, she ran her fingers along the underside. Her breath caught as her fingers connected with something. Stuck between the planks was a small piece of paper. Rupert's receipt from *Lafitte's*. With fire in her eyes, she held it up for Lucille and Ernest to see. She had no doubt that Rupert had stuffed it there as a breadcrumb for her to follow. But what on earth did it mean?

Chapter 15

"What *is* that?" asked Lucille staring at the receipt in Dodo's hand.

"It's the bill for our meal at *Lafitte's Blacksmith Shop*. Rupert must have stuffed it there somehow while they were grabbing him—it could be a clue to where he was taken." She cursed the fact that she had allowed her fears to impede her methodology.

"I should have made a thorough search of the patio before we went to see Rigatti," said Dodo. "In any other case, that is exactly what I would have done. We've wasted so much time." She wrung her hands.

"Don't go down the road of what-ifs, sugar. No good is at the end of that street." Lucille pulled Dodo into her arms for a quick, comforting hug. "Your heart is driving you instead of your head. It's only natural." She took the receipt from Dodo's hand.

"That's enough dilly-dallying, y'all. Let's go!" She ran back into the street to hail another taxi.

"We'll need to do some surveillance first," whispered Ernie, urgently, as they piled into the cab. He had served as a wingman in the Great War. "You can't just go bursting in without knowing the situation on the inside."

"You're right," said Dodo. "That is what I would do with any other case. I can't think straight because I'm so close to this one."

"I suggest we stop the taxi a block from *Lafitte's* and approach gradually like any other tourist. It's an odd place to hide him because it will be swarming with people. But since it's an old smuggler's haunt, I think there might be a secret room."

"Now you're thinkin'!" declared Lucille. "Or maybe they just kept him there overnight until it opened."

Dodo's heart fell off a cliff. "Oh, don't say that!"

Lulu gripped her arm. "We'll find him, sugar."
Let's hope he's still alive when we do!

"Stop here," commanded Lulu. The taxi driver pulled into the curb.

The hot sun was at its peak. A drop of sweat tracked down Dodo's back as she gaped at *Lafitte's*. All the doors were closed, no tourists hanging around outside. *Strange.* As she watched, a couple walked to one of the doors, they read something posted on it and walked away.

"Let me go," said Lulu. "You two are a little…obvious."

Dodo and Ernie stood in the shade of a large tree. Lucille pulled her hat down over her eyes and approached the historic building. It took all of Dodo's willpower not to rush over and break the door down. Lulu stopped, read the notice pinned to the door, and sauntered back.

"It's closed. The sign says, 'Closed until further notice'."

Ernie turned to Dodo. "This is most fortunate, m'lady. We are free to observe and surveille."

"What if the kidnappers are still in there? We don't wanna tip them off," warned Lucille.

"I performed this type of task in the war," explained Ernie. "Let me go first to get the lay of the land. I'll report back, and we can devise a plan together."

Marching in place, Dodo felt the irrational impulse to chew her nails, a habit she had conquered in her youth.

"Child, you need to calm down," cautioned Lucille, placing a soothing hand on Dodo's shoulder. "We need you to focus that cunnin' mind of yours."

"That's easier said than done," Dodo replied. "I've worked on cases involving family members and close friends before, but this…this is altogether different. I'm absolutely terrified that I will fail Rupert."

"Hush your mouth! You are the best little detective this side of the Mississippi and don't you forget it! Worryin' like that's like sitting in a rocking chair. It don't get you no further down the road."

"I'll try not to."

After what seemed like an eternity, Ernie strolled back, eyes gleaming. "As far as I can see, it's empty."

Finally, Dodo could act. "Let's storm the castle. I have my skeleton keys. We can break in."

Without waiting for anyone to deter her, she hurried over to one of the old doors. They were shutter-like, and the lock was extremely old and flimsy. The other two stood, forming a shield while she fiddled with the latch. Within seconds, it clicked and they all slipped inside pulling the door closed behind them. Dodo put a finger to her lips. The other two nodded.

Creeping on tiptoe, the three of them inspected every inch of the small blacksmith's, even the storage room beyond the counter.

Nothing.

The demons of despair began to circle again and Dodo flopped onto a chair next to a large oak cupboard, fighting back tears and rising panic. If they were too late, if Rupert died because she could not do her job…How she wished they had never come.

Hardly aware of Lucille and Ernie discussing their next move, Dodo dropped her head to her hands. Eyes closed, she became aware of a slight breeze flitting across her legs in the stifling heat. They were inside and all the doors and windows were closed. Where could it be coming from? She leapt up, carefully examining the outside of the cupboard. It was decidedly narrow in depth. *Too narrow*. She pulled sharply on the ornate, brass handle. *Locked!* Removing her skeleton keys for the second time, she made short shrift of the antique lock and tugged.

"What the—?"

The so-called cupboard was actually a disguised door to a hidden, windowless room!

Taking a step inside, her hopes fell for the thousandth time. *Empty!* She kicked a pile of rubbish in frustration. A small, clean card dislodged. Bending low, she turned it over. *Rupert's calling card!* Her throat made a knot, and she held the clue to her heart.

Ernie and Lucille stood in the doorway to the secret room.

"He was here!" Dodo held out the card. "Perhaps he left another crumb." Dropping to her haunches, she searched carefully through the refuse, spreading out each paper and wrapper until she was left with one piece, a red ticket stub. Hands trembling, she turned it over. A used ticket to the riverboat. Frantically, she searched for the date. The day they had taken the trip with Lucille and Beau!

"Look! His ticket for the steamboat. I think he's trying to tell me they took him to the port."

"Maybe, maybe," murmured Lucille.

"I know it!" cried Dodo.

By the strange way Lucille regarded her, Dodo knew she must appear manic. She didn't care.

"Okay. You two head over there and I'll go find Beau. We might need reinforcements."

Dodo couldn't help herself. "What if Beau kidnapped Rupert?"

Lucille belly laughed. "Really, honey? I'm goin' to excuse your baseless accusation because you're afraid. But I know Beau pretty well and I'd stake my life on the fact that he plays no part in this kidnappin'."

Dodo shook her head like a horse fending off a fly. "Of course, not! I'm so sorry. I'm not thinking straight."

"Hush up! I don't blame you, sugar. If it was someone I loved, I'd be a sorry mess too. You go on and we'll meet you at the port soon as we can."

"How far is it to walk?" Dodo asked.

"Coupla miles, but in this heat…I'd take a taxi or a tram."

They parted ways and as Dodo and Ernie walked back to the main street, a tram stopped. They barely made it. Dodo too nervous to talk, stared out the window.

Arriving at the port, Dodo headed straight for the coffee shop, Ernie in her wake. Spotting the redheaded waitress, she marched through the café.

"Hello again, miss," said the girl. "Coffee?" Nellie peered behind her at Ernie, brow furrowing.

"No time for coffee today, Nellie. You know the port pretty well, don't you?"

"Lived here all my life, miss."

"Are there any secret places or abandoned warehouses where you could hide a person?"

Appearing as if she were going to drop the tray, Ernie reached out to steady it.

"Uh—well..." She bounced her head. "There's the smuggler's cave at the far end of the proper port. Least, that's what we used to call it as kids. It's a cave dug into the mud with a sheet of metal for a door, covered with sticks. It's easy to miss unless you're looking for it."

Dodo turned to go.

"Wait!" cried the waitress. "There's a small, abandoned coal bunker on this side of the port. They built a bigger one ten years ago and just left the old one. You could hide someone there."

"Miss Boothe!" The manager had appeared and was approaching them like a ship in full sail.

Dodo reached into her handbag and took out two dollars. "It's my fault," she explained to the manageress. "I needed some information and Miss Boothe was *so* helpful last time." She flashed the money. "You can split this for your time. Thank you."

Before the older woman could complain, she and Ernie headed for the door.

"An old bunker," she repeated. They began searching the dockside, Dodo holding back tears as their efforts proved fruitless.

"Here!" shouted Ernie from behind a tree. Hurrying over, she saw that the tree hid the concrete bunker from view. She reached down to take off her shoes.

"Allow me," insisted Ernie, removing his jacket. Hauling himself up, the rough wall scraping his leather shoes in the process, he quickly reached the top and balanced with his hips while heaving up a large, iron door.

"Mr. Danforth!" Ernie's voice ricocheted around the empty hole. "It's dark as a thunder cloud," he called to her over his shoulder. "I need to let my eyes adjust."

Dodo was scratching the back of her hands mindlessly as she waited, thankful for the light lacy gloves.

A loud clanging accompanied Ernie's descent to the ground. "I'm sorry to report that nothing and no one is in there." He grabbed his jacket and slung it over his shoulder.

Each failure was chipping away at her confidence, but Ernie was already off, beating a path to the far side of the port. She had never hated the British stiff upper lip more. Taking a deep breath, she ploughed after him, through the busy port, trying not to fall to pieces. She couldn't afford that luxury.

A steamboat was getting ready to leave and a large group of people surged forward to board. Dodo and Ernie were swimming an upstream battle.

Once through, they scoured every tree and overgrown bush. *Nothing.*

"Let's try again, m'lady," said Ernie, sweat showing through his white shirt. "I fear we were too hasty."

She wanted to scream that all was lost and that everything they were doing was a colossal waste of time. A needle in a haystack. Instead, she renewed her faith in the hope that they would find Rupert alive and joined Ernie in the search.

115

"Over here! I think I found it."

Dodo rushed over. Just as Nellie had warned, it was camouflaged with sticks and leaves.

"Do you think we should wait for Beau?" Ernie asked. "We don't know who we might find on the other side."

"I don't care," wailed Dodo. "I am so full of anger I could fight Goliath himself. Let's go!"

She yanked the jagged metal edge of the makeshift door. It did not budge. Ernie moved beside her and they heaved together. The dainty gloves ripped as the door wrenched open, and they both stumbled as it finally gave way.

Ernie motioned for her to scramble to the sides to see if anyone came out. When no one appeared, Dodo surged forward.

Damp, dark, and dank.

Blinded after the bright sunshine, she moved forward, arms out straight, and tripped over something soft. Crouching, she felt legs bound with strong rope. Her heart leapt to her throat. "Rupert?"

No response.

Her stomach twisted. She was too late. He was dead after all.

Tears dripping from her nose, she shifted position, finding his face with her hands. Tracing his Patrician nose and rugged jaw with her finger, she jerked. He was warm. *Alive!* Feeling a cloth gag, she tore it from his mouth, shaking him gently. "Rupert!"

"Uggh." He began to rouse and she had to restrain herself from crushing him to her in case he was wounded.

"Uggh."

"Sir!" In that one word, Ernie conveyed a world of relief and concern.

Tenderly, Dodo drew Rupert's dear head onto her knees. His eyelids fluttered.

She kissed them, bathing his face with her tears.

Ernie began to untie the ropes around his feet and wrists. "We'd best get him out of here, m'lady. Who knows when they'll return?"

Placing his hands under Rupert's shoulders, Ernie lifted his torso while Dodo took his feet. Between them, they awkwardly carried his six-foot frame out and into the healing sunshine. Dodo gasped. A large shiner framed one eye and dried blood streaked across his forehead. Goodness only knew what other injuries were hidden by his clothes.

After a brief moment's rest, they lifted him again, struggling as he moaned with pain, heading for the main road. A hundred yards in, they met Lucille and Beau.

Lucille stared at Rupert's lifeless form and her face froze.

"He's alive," Dodo assured her through sobs.

"Thank the heavens!" she clapped, looking up at the sky.

"Here," said Beau. "Let me take him."

"We have a car," said Lucille.

Beau gathered up Rupert as easily as a mother picking up her baby and began striding toward the waiting vehicle. Dodo could barely see as she raised a silent prayer of thanks.

Beau placed Rupert along one of the seats and Lucille, Dodo, and Ernie sat on the opposite side while Beau sat next to the driver. Dodo incessantly stroked Rupert's battered face as he swam in and out of consciousness.

When they finally reached Lucille's house, Beau carried Rupert up to his room and Ernie began to dress the cuts and bruises while Dodo kissed his chapped and broken lips. His eyes finally flickered open.

"Dodo."

As he sunk back into unconsciousness, she dropped her head to his chest and wept.

Chapter 16

It was a long night.

Dodo sat up, hour after agonizing hour, with the insensible Rupert and prayed.

Every few hours he would rouse and call her name then sink back into oblivion. A large and bloody goose egg festered on the back of his head. Additional bruises patterned his ribs, front and back.

As dawn broke, roosters began to crow. Dodo stirred. A noise. Pain shot down her neck as she raised it from the bed.

What had woken her?

She opened swollen, burning eyes to find Rupert watching her.

"Hello," she whispered, relief flooding her senses.

"Hello, gorgeous. You're a sight for sore eyes—wait, make that ribs." He tried to laugh but winced with pain.

She put her fingers to his torn lips.

"Someone hit you on the head and kicked you more than a dozen times."

Rupert reached for her hand. "I remember the blow to the head. I must have been unconscious when they kicked me."

"I don't suppose you remember anything?"

Trying to move his head on the pillow, Rupert blanched. "Not much, Sherlock." He smiled weakly. "You had all gone to bed," he continued, "and I was just enjoying the cooler evening air when two figures came at me from both sides in the darkness and put a bag over my head. I started to struggle but they recommended I not do that, or it would turn out badly for you, Dodo. One of them asked the other about *Lafitte's* and desperately, I reached into my pocket and shoved that receipt into the table before they tied my hands together. I had no idea if that's where they were taking me, but it was all I had to go on. They marched me off the porch and into a car waiting around the corner. Before you ask, I didn't recognize either of their voices, but they spoke in strange French sometimes. But I *can* tell you they were working for someone else."

"You poor man." Dodo ran her fingers lightly up and down his arm.

"I tried to listen to their conversation but most of it didn't make sense. It was a strange mixture of English and French."

"Creole."

"Yes, I think so. Well, they *did* take me to *Lafitte's*. I recognized the smell of the old smithy's that clung to the walls. Do you remember that?"

Dodo nodded. It was embedded into the very stone of the place.

"My blindfold wasn't removed until they shoved me into a small, windowless room. But they kept me tied up. I laid and waited, thinking I might never see you again.

"When they returned, they thrust a bowl of beans and some water at me and untied my wrists, but they covered their faces with bandanas. I guessed it was sometime in the early morning hours. Clutching at straws, I took the opportunity to take out one of my cards and hide it under the rubbish on the floor."

"I found it!" she declared.

"I knew you would, darling! What about the used steamboat ticket?"

"Yes! Oh, Rupert, it's what led us to the port. I stormed the café hoping the waitress knew some places one could hide a person."

"I shouldn't have doubted you, sweetheart. Though I must confess there were times I felt that all was lost."

"Me too," she admitted. "Ernie and Lucille literally had to push me to use my sleuthing skills even as I was surrendering to depression."

"I don't mind telling you I've never been so scared in my life. I didn't know if they had been commissioned to kill me or just scare us."

Dodo shivered. "Let's not dwell on 'what-ifs'. You're here, safe."

He squeezed her hand. "Well, even though the French was a dialect, I did recognize the word 'port' and the ticket was a last-ditch effort before they bound my hands again. I didn't have a clue if that's where they were actually going to take me, but I was desperate."

"I'm so glad you did," she murmured.

"When the goons came back to get me, they replaced the blindfold. I guessed it was still dark because it would be difficult to move a prisoner in daylight. Before we went into that cave, I could hear the water. I knew I was near the river. But I worried they would leave me there to die, so I tried to fight back, butting them with my head and shoulders—at that point I had nothing left to lose. That's when they struck me on the back of the head and the lights went out."

Covering her face with both hands, she felt Rupert's fingers touch her skin.

"Don't cry, my darling. It's over now and I have something very important to ask you."

She moved her hands, wiping her cheeks. His features serious, her heart skittered.

"Did they ruin my good shoes?"

Her face split into a watery grin. "I would slap you if you weren't so fragile."

The dawn light highlighted the rough stubble on his chin and her battered heart caught. She realized more than ever that life would not be worth living without him.

Taking her moist hand, he weaved his long fingers between hers.

"Will you marry me, Dodo?"

She started.

A single tear trickled down his whiskered cheek. "Before they knocked me out, I had a lot of time to think and I realized what a perfect fool I've been. What have I been waiting for? The perfect house to present you? The right time of year? The ideal ring? All my reasons for waiting seemed totally idiotic when faced with the fact that I was going to die. I promised God that if He saved me, I would waste no more time. I would ask you right away. And He did."

"Yes."

"Yes?"

"Yes."

"Seeing this thrashed, mess of a human hasn't made you change your mind?"

She leaned down to kiss his split lips, the raw skin sharp against her own, then whispered against them. "Nope."

"I don't have a ring."

"I don't care."

"I may not be presentable for several months."

"I would marry you tomorrow if it wouldn't hurt my family's feelings—bandages, crutches and all."

"I don't deserve you."

"You do. I do. We do."

A gentle knock was followed by the entrance of Lizzie who immediately backed out. "I apologize, m'lady."

Dodo sat up. "Come back, Lizzie."

"Really?"

"Really. You are looking at the future Mrs. Danforth."

Lizzie squealed.

Chapter 17

"'Bout time, I'd say," said Lucille on hearing the news. "It's obvious to everyone that you two should be together."

"Did you *really* just say that, Lucille Bassett?" asked Beau, one brow quirked.

Lucille rolled her eyes. "I can't get you to *stop* asking me."

Beau's mouth hitched up on one side. "Would it help if I did?"

Pushing out her voluptuous bottom lip, Lucille gave him a side eye. "I'm getting kinda used to it."

Dodo saw a light switch on in Beau's friendly eyes.

"Alright," said Dodo as they sat around Lucille's dining table. "We have Rupert back, but we're no farther forward in solving Clyde's murder."

"Does Rupert know who took him?" Lucille asked.

"Most of the time he was blindfolded. But he did hear them speak Creole."

"Like half the city," said Lucille, deflated.

"I've thought a lot about what Rigatti said and I believe him," Dodo admitted. "His goal in life is to inspire compliance by creating terror with his violent, very public crimes. As he said, he doesn't do things in secret—it would defeat his main purpose—triggering fear. So, I'm going to cross him off the list.

"But he *did* make a comment that bears further examination. As I recall, he said that though he did not bomb that club himself, the property would tank in value and he would consider snapping it up to open his own club. We should see if anyone has already made an offer on the land. Do you have any way to find that out, Lucille?"

"Sure do, honey. Mack Bailey is a friend of mine and a real estate agent. I could ask him." She winked. "He owes me a favor."

"Excellent!" Dodo wrote the estate agent's name in her notebook to give her hands something to do. Though they had found Rupert, the whole caper had shaken her to the very core.

"If we take Rigatti off the list who else is left?" asked Beau.

She pushed her notebook across the table, using her pencil to point. "Auggie, who speaks Creole, Tucker, Kid, the window washer and—" Dodo raised sheepish eyes— "Beau."

"I understand you have to consider everyone," Beau said with grace, his fingers tapping each other. "But did you not check out my alibi?

"Oh, Beau! I've been so distracted I didn't," she apologized.

"What *is* your alibi?" asked Lucille,

Head still facing Dodo, his eyes slid to Lucille and back. "We had a *servicin'* problem out by Lake Pontchartrain. Oohwee! It was a doozie! I had to go in person and sweet talk the lady of the house to assure her we'd have everythin' in hand faster than a greased pig. I arrived at her house near on five o'clock and didn't leave till nine. She was none too happy. Those workers'll tell you I didn't leave the whole time." He wiggled those big eyebrows. "I like to lead my men from the front in a crisis. Then I had to go and…freshen up." He batted his lashes like an old lady, which made Dodo smile.

Lucille was not smiling.

"You only have men on the list," said Ernie. "But a woman could hire someone to do her dirty work."

"You're right, but remember, the actual killer would have to be someone Clyde knew, because there were no signs of forced entry or a fight," Dodo reminded them. "So, it's unlikely."

123

"What about this mysterious window washer?" Beau said. "He was definitely there because the neighbor saw him."

"I've been thinking about that," said Dodo. "And I believe the window washing incident is connected to the elusive package. Where is it? Eula Mae knew nothing about it, but the neighbor handled it and hand delivered it to Clyde. But it was addressed to his mother, so maybe he didn't open it. Let's imagine there was something compromising in the package, like photographs— Miss Frannie suggested that herself— that someone didn't want Eula Mae to see. What better way to get a look inside the house and check that no one was home without entering, than pretending to wash the windows. Since Eula Mae never locks her back door, it would be an easy matter to dash in, retrieve the package once it was spotted, then pack up the ladder and go on your merry way. They could not have known that Clyde usually washed the windows."

"It's a good theory but how can you check it?" asked Lucille.

"I can't at the moment. Instead, I'm going to go out on a limb and suggest that it's not connected to the murder at all. The fact that it happened the same day as the death of Clyde has put it under the microscope, but I think it's a false connection and a waste of our resources at this point. If we have no success in our other lines of inquiry, we can come back to it later."

"Okay," said Lucille, her intonation laden with doubt. "You're the expert."

"You don't have the stowaway on your list," said Lizzie.

"Oh, you don't know! So much has happened that I forgot to tell you, Lizzie. We found him! The blood Clyde thought he saw was actually a birth mark. The man is here to find work with his brother and couldn't afford to pay his passage. It could all be a big lie, but Clyde would definitely have been scared of him had he entered the house because we know from the waitress at the coffee shop that he was frightened when Clyde saw him slip out of the boat."

Dodo placed a check mark next to Tucker's name. "Tell me more about Tucker Dawson. He has three sons and owns several clubs and wants to buy yours. What else?"

Beau's nostrils flared.

"He's nice enough to me but I have long suspected him of havin' ties to the mobsters," admitted Lucille. "His family were poor as dirt but by the time he was twenty he had enough money to open a club."

Dodo remembered Tucker's claim that he was able to put some money aside when he was young. This flew in the face of Lucille's testimony that they were too poor to save anything.

"It was fishy," continued Lucille. "But me and Daddy were just gettin' our start and we'd perform at his club. I'm kinda in his debt 'cos that's where we were discovered and signed with a record label."

Beau's fist tapped the table. "*That's* why you give him the time of day?"

Lucille shrugged. "I feel obliged. Without him, I might still be a struggling singer."

A smile of satisfaction spread over Beau's face like a sunrise and he slid a beefy arm across the back of Lucille's chair.

"What are Tucker's sons like?" Dodo asked.

"Rough around the edges but that's to be expected with a father like that and no mama," replied Lucille. "She died when they were quite young. They became more...primitive after the loss of her influence. Sad really. She was a nice girl—Ginny Gervais. We were all *really* surprised when she married Tucker."

"It might be time to see if those boys have an alibi," remarked Dodo.

"And how are you going to do that?" asked Beau.

Dodo arched her brow. "Are you offering?"

"I can do some sniffing around, if y'all want me to."

"Be careful," warned Lucille. "We know the murderer will stop at nothin' to try to put an end to our meddlin'."

"Are you concerned for my health, Mizz Bassett?" crooned Beau. In answer, she swatted his arm but he still looked like the cat who got the cream.

"I wish we could know if Tucker's finances are as healthy as he would have us believe," murmured Dodo.

Raising her hands to the sky, Lucille declared. "Oh, sugar! The bank manager owes me a favor too. I should be able to get you that information by this afternoon."

"Very good." Dodo went back to her list. "Next is…Auggie. He's piqued my interest since our little adventure because he speaks Creole *and* owns *Lafitte's*."

"He may have the charm of a skunk at a lawn party, but I've never seen him be violent," said Lucille. "And what would be his motive?"

Dodo had to agree. "I haven't come up with one yet, however, he does check some of the other boxes. He was a familiar face to Clyde *and* he was at the club that night. He could have easily slipped out and done the deed and been back before anyone noticed." Her eyes went to the word 'rat'. "If he was behind the bombing, Clyde may have seen him or something."

Lucille shook her head. "Anythin' is possible, I suppose." It was clear she didn't believe it. "You think there's a link between the bombing and the murder?"

"Yes! There's an explosion that destroys a business, then someone defaces Eula Mae's door with graffiti that says 'rat'. I don't like coincidences. And the very word insinuates that someone was worried Clyde was going to spill the beans. So, if this *is* all connected to the bombing, then we have to draw the conclusion that Clyde may have seen something he shouldn't. The graffiti was definitely a warning. The neighbor stated that Clyde was washing the graffiti off so it didn't upset his mother. But if my theory is

126

correct, it's probable that he knew exactly what it meant and didn't want Eula Mae asking questions." She drew a circle around Auggie's name. "If it looked like Clyde wasn't going to heed the warning, the murderer would have felt compelled to silence him permanently." Dodo looked up from the notebook. "Could you ask your bank manager about Auggie?"

"Sure."

Dodo hesitated. "There is one more person."

All eyes moved to her notebook.

"Kid."

Lucille laughed out loud. "You're not serious."

"Not really, but I've learned you have to consider everyone. He *does* speak Creole—"

Lucille interrupted. "He's also chained to my kitchen!"

"He never uses the lavatory? Or has a coffee break?" Dodo asked.

"Well, sure. But the very idea…" Lucille couldn't even finish the sentence.

"Does he have no vices?"

Lizzie and Ernie sat wide-eyed as the atmosphere crackled with scorn.

"No!" But even as she said it, a spark in Lucille's eye said otherwise. "Well, he plays cards with a group of old friends, but it's child's play. They've been playin' for thirty years. Everyone plays cards. I dabble too."

"Point taken." Dodo snapped her notebook shut. "Let's focus on the others for now. We'll regroup here this afternoon before Lucille has to go back to the club. Any objections?"

Chapter 18

Uncomfortable with leaving Rupert alone in the house in case the kidnappers tried again, Dodo, Lizzie, and Ernest stayed at Lucille's home while she and Beau left to follow up on alibis and banking and real estate matters.

Beau carried Rupert to the sofa in the front facing lounge before he left. Unable to be parted from him, Dodo sat on the same sofa with his feet on her lap while Lizzie perched close by, darning socks, on a pouf near his head. As Ernie dressed Rupert's cuts with rubbing alcohol and faithfully administered aspirin, Dodo was of the mind that a professional nurse could not have met Rupert's needs any better.

The fan was turning at full speed, the French windows slightly ajar to create a crosswind, when they heard the door. Dodo tensed and Ernie, straddling his legs in a half crouch, lifted his fists, ready to do battle.

"It's just me!" sang Lucille, gliding into the room in a flurry of bright chiffon. "Have I got news for y'all!" She sank into one of the overstuffed armchairs cooling herself with a pretty fan. "I could do with some iced tea," she hinted.

"I'll get it," said Lizzie.

"Well?" asked Dodo.

"Y'all were right! It appears our Tucker is totally strapped for cash. Poor as Job's turkey! He took out loans at the bank against the equity from his first three clubs to buy two more but they're not makin' enough to pay Rigatti *and* make his loan payments."

"Why wouldn't he just ask Rigatti for the money?" croaked Rupert.

"Rigatti may be a violent criminal but he's not stupid. If he believes it's throwin' good money after bad, he won't do it. And who knows? Tucker may be embarrassed to let Rigatti know he's in trouble. Male ego and all that jazz."

"That provides a solid motive for something, but not for killing Clyde," said Dodo puffing air through her lips. "Unless…"

"Unless what?" demanded Lucille.

"It's just fumes of an idea right now. I need to let it marinate just a little before I put it on the table."

Beau burst into the living room. Everyone gasped.

"Beau! Saints alive, man! You can't be doin' that when there are kidnappers around," scolded Lucille. "You need to announce yo'self well before you come in, do ya hear?"

Beau put a hand over his heart. "Apologies, Lucille, but I have some scoop that y'all are going to find mighty interestin'." He sat on the arm of Lucille's chair, his eyes jumping back and forth.

"Out with it then!" cried Lucille.

"Tucker's boys've been beaten to a pulp by Rigatti's men. By all accounts, they was tryin' to swindle Rigatti by sayin' they were earnin' less than they were so as not to pay such a large extortion payout. Ragatti was madder 'an a hornet."

"That's because they *can't* pay it," confirmed Lucille. "I'm just back from the bank."

"When did this attack on Tucker's boys happen?" asked Dodo.

"Tucker didn't know it at the time, but the day after Clyde was killed," Beau announced. "Probably while he was sittin' in Eula Mae's house."

"That might mean Tucker is smoldering for revenge against Rigatti." said Rupert.

"Oh, and I've confirmed Tucker's alibi for the night of the murder from several of his employees who were there when Rigatti's henchman came to make trouble," added Beau.

129

"Then he has no reason to kidnap me," concluded Rupert.

Dodo tapped her lips. *Think!* It would cost money to pay people to kidnap Rupert. Enough to make it worth their while. Tucker clearly didn't have that kind of cash and as Beau had now confirmed, it seemed neither he, nor his sons, had the opportunity. However, all this might explain why Tucker was so desperate to buy *Lulu's*. Lucille's business was making a nice profit and had the potential to rescue his other clubs. Dodo took Tucker off her list.

"You've done an amazing job," said Dodo. "Tucker is certainly in trouble, but at the moment, I agree with Rupert. I see no connection to Clyde."

"Okay, how about *this?*" began Lucille. "My real estate friend said Auggie made an offer for the *Hurdy Gurdy* the day after the bombing."

"Now, that *is* interesting!" Dodo declared.

"*And* he speaks Creole," added Rupert.

"That's not all," continued Lucille. "Auggie offered half what the land is worth and Frankie accepted the offer."

Dodo's mind whirled. "Let's say Auggie approached Frankie, but he refused to sell. So, Auggie arranged for a little accident. You told me no one was hurt in the explosion, Lucille. Seems like the bomber was careful to strike when the place was empty, which is in line with your opinion that Auggie is not a violent man. He took a chance, or heard through the grapevine, that Frankie was not insured and would need to sell to recoup any of his money." She snapped her head to Lucille. "Is there *any* chance Clyde could have seen someone set the charge at the *Hurdy Gurdy?*"

"No! He's at work until late." She paused. "Wait!" Pointing a finger, she explained, "With all that's happened since, I completely forgot, but I *did* ask Clyde to hurry and take a message to the owner of the *Jockey Club* downtown. They buy our leftover food to use the next evenin', but I'd had a problem with the wholesaler, and we were short that day. It was important to tell the owner that night because he'd have to make other arrangements. Usually, Kid would do that since it's on his way home, but he had to leave right after the club closed for some problem at home. So, I sent Clyde round to the *Jockey Club* at four in the mornin'. Clyde'd have to go right past the *Hurdy* to get there." Her face collapsed. "You don't think *I* got that boy killed, do ya?"

"No one but the murderer is responsible for killing Clyde," declared Dodo.

"But maybe that's why *'rat'* was painted on Eula Mae's door. Clyde must have seen someone who shouldn't have been near the *Hurdy*," guessed Lucille.

Beau took her hand and she didn't pull it away.

Kid appeared in the doorway. "Bernice asked me to bring food by for your lunch."

"That's right nice of you, Kid. Bernice tripped over the step this morning and twisted her ankle," Lucille explained to the rest of the room.

"I left it in the kitchen," said Kid. "I'd better be gettin' back to the club. See y'all later!"

Lizzie stood. "I can put the food on plates and bring it in here, if you'd like."

"Fabulous!" said Lucille. "You're a real treasure, darlin'."

Ernest jumped up. "I'll help."

"Does any of this take your thoughts in a new direction?" Rupert asked Dodo. "Honestly, I can't concentrate on anything with my head banging like this."

"It does!" said Dodo, her head digesting the fresh information. "If Clyde was in the area of the *Hurdy* before the bombing, it puts a whole new twist on things. I think we have to assume he saw who set the blast and that is the person who killed him."

"I doubt Clyde would've put two and two together," said Lucille. "He was just a child in intellect."

"That may be true, but if you're the bomber, it's a risk you can't take. I would say it looks like the saboteur painted the door to scare Clyde into silence, but Clyde must have said or done something that really worried the perpetrator to the point that a quick execution was deemed necessary."

"And you think it was Auggie because he made such a quick bid for the *Hurdy*?" asked Beau.

"Sure is beginning to look that way," declared Lucille.

Chapter 19

That afternoon, Dodo found herself on the way to *Lafitte's* with Lucille and Beau. Lucille had called to see if Auggie was home and been told she could find him at the eatery. Rupert had convinced Dodo to go as he wanted to sleep and assured her that Ernie would fight any would-be kidnappers to the death.

"How do you want to go about this?" asked Beau enroute. "I don't recommend confronting him with an accusation. If he's killed already, we're just asking for trouble."

"I've done a lot of thinking about this and I believe it would just be better to pretend you're interested in buying the *Hurdy Gurdy* during the natural flow of conversation, Beau. Say you've heard it's for sale at a cheap price," suggested Dodo. "Gauge his reaction. The topic will put him on his guard, though I doubt he'll admit to purchasing it already. Looks bad given the circumstances."

"He *does* know I have that kind of money," said Beau. "I think I can pull it off."

"Perfect," said Dodo, her veins pumping adrenaline as they headed into battle. "Once a suspect is off balance, I've found that traps work well. Guilty people are hyper aware, hyper on edge, and don't act rationally. I think if we drop into the conversation that someone has contacted us with information about the bombing and they want to meet in secret at the far end of the north dock at midnight, he'll take the bait."

"That's right in the middle of work for me," Lucille reminded them.

"I think Ernie and I can handle it," Beau assured her. "It's pointless appealing to our police force."

Lucille grabbed his arm. "What if Auggie has a gun?"

Beau pursed his lips. "If I didn't know better, Mizz Bassett, I'd say you're concerned for my welfare again."

Lucille withdrew her hand. "I'd be concerned for anyone if a gun is involved."

The taxi pulled to the curb outside *Lafitte's*.

All at once, Dodo was seized with concern that her amateur accomplices might give them away. "Are you both able to act naturally, as if nothing is wrong? We can't tip Auggie off by anything unusual in our conduct."

Lucille straightened her hat and shoulders. "I've done some acting in my time. Don't you worry, darlin'."

Dodo turned her sights on Beau who shrugged. "My mama told me I was a clown all the time, so I think I'm covered."

"Alright then, it's showtime." Dodo glanced up as they approached the open doors of *Lafitte's*. "Now, imagine I just said something terribly funny."

The pair began to laugh lightly as they pushed through the door of the small restaurant. Dodo shuddered thinking of the last time she had been there but plastered on a smile. The place was full of tourists and Dodo felt the assurance of safety in numbers. They ambled over to the bar still pretending to have found their conversation amusing and each ordered an item from the menu.

Auggie appeared at the door that separated the main room from the kitchen, a look of surprise on his face. Whether it was to see them there or because he was the kidnapper and knew that Rupert had been rescued, she could not tell.

"Lulu! Beau! *Hé là-bas*! And your lovely foreign friend." He called to the people taking the orders. "This one's on the house!"

Lucille dipped her chin and batted her lashes. "Why, thank you! That's mighty generous of you, Auggie."

"Think nothin' of it, Lucille. Please, take a seat." He gestured to a table behind them. "I'll bring it out personally."

Dodo began telling Beau and Lucille about meeting Rupert's parents to prevent a lull in the conversation and to keep her mind off the kidnapping. Within a few minutes, Auggie returned holding their plates.

"Why don't you sit with us a while," Beau suggested. "Do you often wait on tables?"

Auggie's brow knitted. "No, not at all. I was checkin' on inventory when I heard you folks come in. I'll gladly sit."

They talked of the weather and the funeral and Auggie said all the right things. After ten minutes, Beau briefly alluded to interest in buying the *Hurdy*, but Auggie hardly batted an eye.

Dodo flared her eyes at Lucille to indicate they should move into more dangerous territory.

"The darndest thing happened today," began Lucille, placing her chin in the palm of her hand, a coy expression indicating she had gossip to share.

"And what would that be?" asked Auggie, leaning forward in his chair.

"You know little Miss Sherlock here is investigatin' Clyde's murder to give poor Eula Mae some justice. It ain't no secret," she added. "Well, we got the strangest phone call today from someone disguising their voice."

Auggie's smile vanished and he slid to the very edge of his seat. "What did they say?"

"It was some kook claimin' they had information, but they insisted on meetin' us at midnight at the far end of the north dock. Declared it needed to be all hole and corner because they feared for their life. Can you believe it?"

Beau chimed in. "I told Mizz Dorchester, here, that it was far too suspicious and she shouldn't go. If someone wants to make a statement they should do it in the bright light of day."

135

"So, you're not goin'?" asked Auggie with a phony smile, sharp at the edges.

"I've considered Beau's reasoning, and I think he's right. When we don't show up tonight, they'll have to come to us during business hours," replied Dodo.

"I believe that's very wise," responded Auggie. "Very wise." He looked at the clock. "Now, you must excuse me, I have matters to attend to. *A plus tard.*"

As he left the table, Lucille leaned forward. "I think—"

Dodo gave a tight shake of the head to warn Lucille to think before she spoke. "Why I'd *love* to see your cathedral," said Dodo with a little more enthusiasm than necessary.

She began to regale them with the tale of her journey across the Atlantic as they put some distance between themselves and *Lafitte's.*

"That's far enough," Dodo said, finally. "I was worried he'd try to listen to us from behind the door to the kitchen."

"Do you think he took the bait?" asked Beau.

"We'll find out at midnight."

Dodo was torn. She feared for Rupert, injured at the house, but desperately wanted to be part of the grand finale of her case. And since Ernie had been conscripted into helping Beau, it left Rupert too vulnerable.

"Nonsense," said Lucille. "*Smokey Syncopation* has one set at ten o'clock, then I'll send Cy and Dex over to keep Mr. Rupert and your little Lizzie company. It's all set. No one would be stupid enough to try anything in a house full of people.

"She's right," said Rupert whose black eye had doubled in size. "You need to be there, Dodo. But I must insist you stay far away from the action, darling. Beau is right, Auggie could bring a gun to the rendezvous."

136

She wavered. "If you're sure Dex and Cy are coming…I think I will go."

Lizzie looked like she'd seen a ghost. "A gun?"

Ernie took both her hands. "I've been in worse in the war, Lizzie. I know how to be careful. What is one man against so much battle experience?"

"One man with a pistol," she retorted.

"I'll grant you that, but I'll be extra careful. I've discussed a plan of action with Mr. Buckley. Though not foolproof, it will enable us to use the element of surprise to our advantage."

At eleven, Dodo, Beau, and Ernie made their way over to the end of the north dock. They had brought a Mardi Gras mannequin dressed in black and placed it near a tree on a grassy area. They did not need the model to speak. Auggie's arrival alone would condemn him. Beau and Ernie were hidden behind some brush, wielding baseball bats and Dodo, dressed in black slacks and shirt with sensible shoes, was secreted several hundred yards off behind a pile of barrels on the wharf.

There was nothing left to do but wait.

Fortunately, an almost full moon shone in a partly cloudy sky; not enough light to betray the mannequin for what it was, but just enough to convince the beholder that it was an actual human.

Dodo shivered, not because it was cold, but because she was brim full of anticipation. She looked at her watch. A quarter past eleven. Why did time go so slowly when one was impatient?

The port and the river were quiet; only the gentle lapping against the dock making any sound. The birds were all in bed. Being too tightly wound, she had been unable to eat anything for dinner.

She tried breathing deeply. One, two, three, four. She reached a hundred.

Only half past eleven!

Time for another pastime. She examined how the moon's light formed an ethereal pathway across the flowing water.

Footsteps.

Dodo melted into the shadow of the barrels, shrinking as low as possible, heart thudding loudly.

As the figure passed her striding confidently, she moved up so that only her eyes rose above the edge of the barrels. Reaching the grass and noticing the mannequin, the dark figure slowed to a crawl but as he closed in on the dummy, Beau and Ernie exploded from their hiding place.

"Ahhhhh!" Auggie screamed like a little girl.

Once Beau and Ernie had securely bound him, Dodo advanced from the wharf. Terrified, Auggie was speechless.

"What do you have to say for yourself?" asked Dodo.

Finding his voice at last, Auggie cried, "What is the meaning of this? I was just out for a stroll and these…these men attacked me."

"Do I look stupid, Mr. Benoit? You came here tonight with the intention of discovering what secret our informant possessed. *You* set the bomb at the *Hurdy Gurdy*."

"I…I…no…no. Not me."

"If we go to your place of residence, we will find no explosive materials?" she demanded.

"Uh, well." Auggie struggled against his bonds, but he was no match for the hulking Beau.

"And I take *great* exception to you kidnapping my fiancé and leaving him to die in a hidden cave—"

"*Non!*"

"Not to mention the murder of a young man who was the gentlest of creatures and his mother's sole companion."

"I DID NOT MURDER CLYDE!" screamed Auggie, real fear strangling his words.

"Then why are you here?"

"Look, I...I...I will cop to the b...b...bomb—I made sure no one got hurt. But you cannot hang the murder or the kidnappin' on me. I would never. *Non!* You *must* believe me."

A flicker of doubt emerged in Dodo's conscience. "You killed Clyde because he saw you at the *Hurdy* before the bombing."

"Impossible! I took no part in the actual bombing myself. I hired others. Please, you *must* believe me."

"Who?" she ordered.

"I don't know. I thought it'd be better done anonymously. I paid them a king's ransom through a third party. The less I knew the better. That way, I thought it couldn't lead back to me."

"Why?" Beau's deep voice was charged with concern for Frankie.

"I overheard Frankie say he'd let his insurance slip but hoped to sell for a high price next year when he retired. It was wrong."

"I know the police won't care," spat Dodo. "They assume it was Rigatti, but what are you going to do to make amends to Frankie?"

"I...I..."

"You're gonna help him rebuild," boomed Beau, causing Auggie to jerk his head. "And if you don't, I'll tell Rigatti it was you trying to steal his turf."

Even in the dim light, Dodo could see Auggie's terrified face drain of any color that was left.

"Promise?" bellowed Beau.

"Yes, yes. I promise. Can you let me go?"

At a sign from Beau, Ernie checked Auggie's pockets and withdrew a small pistol.

"Well, well, well. What have we here?" asked Beau.

"Keep it. Just let me go."

"What do you think, Mizz Dorchester?" asked Beau.

"I think we would be fools to release him," she replied.

"Agreed. But you're in luck, Auggie. We won't throw your miserable body in the river."

Beau and Ernie slung him to the ground, and they all marched away as a grown man sobbed for his sins.

Chapter 20

Curled tight as a coil, Dodo was surprised to find Rupert still awake, talking quietly with Cy and Dex. Beau had gone directly to the club to fill in Lucille.

"How'd it go?" asked Dex.

Lizzie had dropped off in the easy chair, delicate mending still in her hands. She roused.

"Perfectly," declared Dodo. "Like the final scene of a play unfolding right before our eyes."

"You did it again, darling."

"Not really." Dodo flopped to the sofa as Ernie placed an arm around the sleepy Lizzie. "Unfortunately, it wasn't quite the ending we were anticipating."

"What?" Rupert hoisted himself up using his arms, flinching from the pain. "Tell me everything."

Adrenaline fueling their chatter, Dodo and Ernie replayed the events of the evening while their audience listened in disbelief.

Holding his sides as he chuckled, Rupert said, "He cried like a baby? How I wish I could have been there."

"That weasel always did have cotton between the ears," announced Cy, pounding a cushion. "I woulda paid good money to see that!"

"But the thing is, Auggie admitted to the bombing but insisted he didn't kill Clyde or orchestrate your kidnapping."

"And you believe the scoundrel?' asked Dez, thumbing his nose.

"And it was at *Lafitte's* that I was held captive," Rupert reminded her.

"I know, darling," said Dodo, the nervous energy all blown out. "He may have allowed the kidnapper to use his place but there was something in his tone. And it's not like he would be prosecuted or anything. No, it was fear of Lucille's contempt, I think."

"I was there, and I agree with Lady Dorothea," said Ernie. "It was like confessions I heard in the trenches in France. No further need to dissemble."

"Justice for the *Hurdy* but not for young Clyde," sighed Dex.

"Indeed."

The two musicians stood. "We'd best be going so we can catch our last set," said Dex.

Dodo jumped up to embrace them. "I can't thank you enough! I was able to focus all my attention on the task at hand, knowing Rupert was safe, here with you."

"Y'all are welcome. Anytime," said Cy as he and Dex headed for Lucille's front door.

"Do you have any theories?" Rupert asked.

Dodo flung her arms along the back of the sofa. "Not really. Auggie revealed that he paid others to set the explosives, that he didn't even know who they were. I still think somehow Clyde discovered one of them on his way to the *Jockey Club* and became a liability. It's the only thing that makes sense."

"Don't get down on yourself, sweetheart. Your trap did successfully catch a rat."

Rat!

The memory of the ugly graffiti did lend credibility to her current theory, but she was fresh out of leads.

"I'll try to appreciate the win," she sighed as the final dregs of adrenaline drained from her system, leaving her utterly exhausted. "And now, I must go to bed before I fall asleep right here."

"I'll settle Lizzie upstairs then come to attend you, Mr. Danforth," said Ernie.

Rupert nodded. Lizzie gathered up her sewing things in a basket and pushed to her feet, leaning on Ernie.

Once they were gone, Dodo kissed Rupert on the forehead.

"Wait."

Her eyes searched his to find them teeming with expectation and mischief. She quirked a brow.

"I can't get down on one knee," he admitted. "Hold out your hand."

As she did, he slipped a gold piece of tassel tied in a circle onto her finger.

She gasped.

"Lizzie was mending one of your dresses and a tassel loosened and fell to the floor. I stole it while she wasn't looking."

Dodo's gaze misted. "I love it."

"We'll go to Hatton Garden and get a proper one as soon as I'm better."

"It will not be any dearer to me than this," she said, placing her lips on the substitute.

She shimmied onto the couch where he lay, and placed her head on his shoulder as he gently stroked her hair.

"Oh, excuse me, sir!" declared Ernie as he returned.

"It's alright, Ernie," said Dodo. "I need to go upstairs, anyway." She pulled herself up and headed for the door. "Thank you," she said, placing her hand on the door frame to steady her weary body. As she turned back for one more glance at Rupert, her eyes settled near the hand with its substitute ring. She stopped short. A smudge of reddish brown on the white frame stared back at her. Her mind pulled up an image of the same stain on the back door frame at Eula Mae's.

And on the back of Clyde's neck.

Fatigue, shock, confusion and elation all crashed together and she grabbed the doorframe again to steady herself.

"What is it Dodo?" asked Rupert.

"I know who did it."

Chapter 21

Up with the lark and nursing a banging headache, nothing could stop Dodo now that she had unraveled the mystery and solved the riddle.

Lucille's cook, Bernice, had given Dodo a strange concoction to drink with breakfast that she guaranteed would deal with the headache within one hour.

Dodo had shared her preliminary deductions with Rupert and Ernie before finally going to bed the night before but had refrained from letting the cat out of the bag with Lucille until she had dotted all her i's and crossed all her t's. She could still be wrong.

She and Lizzie were planning to travel downtown alone, a decision which scandalized Ernie who insisted on coming with them. In spite of her swollen ankle, Bernice had taken up vigil outside Rupert's room holding a large, solid iron frying pan and daring anyone to try and hurt him on her watch.

The three of them were now on a streetcar headed to Buddy's neighborhood.

"Do you think his mother will allow him to help?" asked Ernie.

Dodo tightened her jaw. "I'm going to offer a considerable sum that I hope will erase any misgivings."

They hopped off and Dodo recognized the tree where she and Rupert had taken shelter from the blazing sun. From there it was easy to recognize the correct house. The street was almost bare as it was still quite early, and she hoped Buddy would still be asleep after a night running errands for Lucille and not off gallivanting.

Dodo rapped hard on the battered front door. The sharp strains of a mother yelling for someone to see who it was, muffled its way through the wood. Eventually, a cute girl of about four years appeared before them, sucking her thumb.

Dark eyes big as plates, the thumb suspended in mid-air, she was shocked into stunned silence.

"Can you get your mother, please?" asked Dodo.

The girl's gaze lingered on Dodo's dress as she backed away, finally running.

Buddy's pretty mother appeared, holding the baby in her arms and pulling at the top of her dress. Lines of fatigue streaked her beautiful face. Again, her expression was curiosity laced with defiance or fear.

"My name is Miss Dorchester and my friends and I are associates of Miss Lucille Bassett."

A hint of a change in attitude appeared on the mother's features. She brushed at her hair that was mostly caught up in a bright scarf the colors of ripe citrus.

"I understand that Buddy runs errands for Miss Bassett," continued Dodo.

"That's right," she said, her voice like windchimes. Dodo wondered if she had also once been a lead singer in the church choir. "Mizz Bassett is *real* good to us."

Making progress.

"I have come to ask permission to send Buddy on another errand. For me. Would that be alright?" She withdrew several dollars from her pocket and the young mother's eyes locked onto the bills.

"What do y'all want him to do?" The baby let out a tiny cry and the odor of sweet syrup wafted through the short hall.

"I just need him to take a note to someone a little south of Miss Bassett's club."

Another girl of about seven appeared. Clutching her mother's legs, she peeked around them. "Buddy does that all the time anyway. No need for y'all from yonder to come on over here."

Dodo shrugged. "I want to make sure I do things properly." She handed Buddy's mother three dollars.

"I'll fetch 'im. He's a late riser 'cos 'e helps out Mizz Bassett."

"Of course. We'll wait for him under the tree." Dodo pointed.

As the door closed, the gentle tones became more shrill, calling up the stairs for Buddy.

Within five minutes he was there, sleep still clinging to his face. "Y'all need somethin'?"

"I do." Dodo wasn't sure he could read and didn't want to embarrass him, so told him the mission.

"Easy! I goes there all the time! If it ain't this, it's that," he said, bouncing along the road to the streetcar stop.

Having hoped this might be the case so that his presence would not raise suspicion, she asked, "Is there anyone in the house that speaks Creole?"

"Yes, ma'am. Two 'n them daughters married Creoles. Pierre and Pascal."

This was good news indeed.

Chapter 22

The stage for the *dénouement* was set.

Regretfully, Rupert would not be able to attend, but it could not be helped. Lizzie and Ernie accompanied Dodo. Lucille and Beau were already there, antsy with anticipation.

Dodo had invited all the major players in the drama to come to *Lulu's* for drinks of cola and to celebrate her engagement—even Rigatti.

The cleaners had left the place spic and span, pine detergent desperately trying to smother the cigarette smoke. Snacks and soda bottles lined the bar.

Eula Mae was the first to arrive, a ghost of her former self but still making an attempt to be social. She shimmied over to Dodo in a bright, peacock blue dress with a matching slouch hat.

"Your fiancé's not really my type anyway," Eula Mae said with a half-hearted cackle. "But I'm happy for you." She swiped a cola from the bar and found a seat in the velvet booth with Lucille and Beau.

As she settled into her seat, Tucker appeared wearing a dark suit with a trilby between his hands, his gaze sweeping nervously back and forth across the room. He nodded to Lucille, who acknowledged him with a half-smile, then wandered over to Dodo.

"I was surprised to get your invite," he said. "I didn't think you liked me."

Dodo raised her shoulders. "I'm far from home, Mr. Dawson, and want to celebrate," she replied.

"Where's the lucky man?" Tucker looked around her.

"He got held up. He'll be here," Dodo lied.

"I came because this town has had enough of sadness these last few days. Thought I could do with something hopeful." Tucker reached for a cola, found an empty booth, and lit up a cigarette.

Dex and Cy arrived and began to play quietly in the background, lending weight to the ruse that this really *was* a party.

Rigatti swaggered into the room, an expensive suit shining in the rays of sunlight coming in from the windows, his good eye roving the room. Dodo felt her skin crawl. Locking onto her, he strode across. "Is this really about Lucille signin' on?" he said with that raspy voice that grated so much.

"I told you, it's to celebrate my engagement," she insisted. "I don't know many people in town, and I now believe you aren't responsible for the bombing, so I invited you."

He puckered thin lips and nodded. "I don't need approval from the likes of you."

"Pat, you've been invited to a celebration. Dig up some manners," Beau growled.

The mobster removed a flask from his pocket, took a swig and slid into a booth looking ready to shoot everyone.

Kid pushed through the back door laden with red crawdads and muffalettas, at Dodo's request, and laid them on the bar. He wiped his hands on his dirty apron and made to head back to the kitchen.

"Stay," said Dodo. "Stay and party with us."

His eyes narrowed and he rubbed the damaged ear. At a nod from Lucille and Beau, Kid jumped onto a plush bar stool and chewed on a crawdad.

Dodo stood. "I'd like to thank you all for coming. It's not every day you get engaged, and we wanted to celebrate in spite of everything that's happened."

Ernie clapped and hooted and everyone followed suit, except Rigatti.

"As a bit of a private detective, I celebrate by working out puzzles."

148

A subtle tension eased into the room, darting glances replacing the smiles of only a minute before.

Rigatti made to stand. "This is a set up."

"You'll want to stay, Rigatti," said Beau in his deep, rumbling voice. Rigatti shrugged and sat back down.

"I came to Louisiana to celebrate the life of Lonnie Chapman. A life cut short by a man eaten up with vengeance," began Dodo.

A couple of people shifted in their seats.

"But violence followed me when Clyde was killed far too young."

Eula Mae grabbed her throat, lips trembling.

"Why on earth would anyone kill a young man who was nothing but friendly and cheerful, someone who lit up a darkening world with his innocence, the apple of his mother's eye?" She looked around the room, people shrinking from her gaze.

"I could not rest, especially in this town where the very people you depend on to uphold the law turn a blind eye."

Dodo walked in a tight circle. "Right from the beginning there was so much misdirection. Strange window washers, missing packages, a threatening defacement of Eula Mae's front door, a huge explosion that damaged a club to extinction. Were any of these things significant or were they distractions from the murder?"

"My front door?" asked Eula Mae with confusion. Lucille reached out, placing her hand over Eula Mae's and whispering in her ear.

"Guilt ate at the conscience of the murderer and fearing that I would succeed in identifying who had carried out this despicable crime, the killer made a mistake. He kidnapped my fiancé, leaving a threatening note that if I did not desist, he would kill Rupert."

Murmurs broke out across the room.

149

"The murderer underestimated me." She spun around. "Instead of intimidating me, this cruel act fueled my anger and I vowed to bring him, or her, to some kind of justice."

She walked over to a chair and sat. Crossing her legs, she placed her hands on her knee as silence choked the room.

"There were few clues at the scene. Bruises big enough to suggest a male killer, no real signs of a struggle, indicating that Clyde knew his attacker, and a wood varnish stain both on Clyde's neck and on the back doorframe. Not much. Couple that with a doctor who couldn't wait to get back to his bootleg whiskey and an investigator whose heart was with those who gave him hush money, and this crime could have fallen through the cracks. If only the killer hadn't got rattled and kidnapped Rupert, I may have been forced to leave the United States before solving the murder."

The guests were looking at their hands or the tables, discomfort poking out of them like spikes.

"Due to his quick thinking, my friends and I were able to find Rupert alive. Broken, but alive. Though blindfolded and unable to give a description of his jailers, Rupert was able to tell us that his assailants were Creole speakers. As far as I knew, only Auggie Benoit fit that description and I concentrated my attention on him. However, though responsible for another serious crime, it became evident that he was not guilty of this one.

"The mysterious window washer remained elusive, the misdelivered package vanished into thin air. But it was the word '*rat*' scrawled across Eula Mae's door that took hold of me and wouldn't let go. It implied that Clyde had been in the wrong place at the wrong time and witnessed the murderer committing another crime. He had to be extinguished in case, in his innocence, he put two and two together and blurted out what he had seen to Eula Mae.

This was Clyde's offense. But who had he seen? What had he seen? All these answers were just out of my reach."

Lulu was watching her carefully.

"Was it Tucker with his slick manner and obvious greed? Was it Auggie who had plans to expand his holdings? Was it Beau who hung around the club and knew Clyde so well? Was it Patrick Rigatti, criminal mastermind and master in chief of the city? And what had the killer done that he was so fearful of discovery?

"Then Lucille remembered that on the night of the bombing, she had sent Clyde to deliver a message to someone downtown and that he would have passed the *Hurdy Gurdy* at close to four in the morning, the night of the explosion. Finally, a piece of evidence that might help in the discovery of a motive for the killing. Clyde's short trip downtown was quickly followed by the taunt scrawled on the front door in dripping paint. Someone was trying to frighten Clyde into silence.

"We all knew the 'how' and now I had a possible 'why', but the 'who'—the most crucial ingredient, still eluded me.

"Then fate stepped in to help me. I discovered a similar reddish-brown stain on a doorframe in Lucille's house that I had seen in Eula Mae's home the night of the murder. At the time, I had assumed it was wood stain. But no one in Lucille's home was staining any furniture. Had the setting at Eula Mae's drawn me to conclude a false assumption? If not stain, what else could it be? Who else had been in the house? I ran through the faces in my mind...and then it hit me."

She paused and the occupants of the room sat rigid like statues.

"But I had to be sure. I had to try to untangle the web of deceit and deviousness that led to this senseless crime. So, I sent a spy to the house of the killer. A spy no one would suspect. And he brought me back the verification I needed."

151

Dodo stood and walked with grace and poise over to the bar.

"Kid, would you hold up your hands?" Alarm cut a path up his features, and she pointed to his middle. "Look at his apron. It appears to be covered in blood, but it's caused by innocuous Cajun spices. Now, look at his fingers. They're stained with the same spices—the spices that caused the print on Eula Mae's door and on the neck of poor Clyde."

Kid hurled himself off the stool but Beau blocked the door.

"Why?" cried Eula Mae, reaching with hands like claws, ready to scratch his eyes from his skull. "Why?"

"It was you Clyde saw fleeing from the scene before the bombing, wasn't it?" Dodo accused.

Rearing back from Eula Mae's frenzied outburst, panicked eyes flashing from person to person and finally settling on the pain and woe in Lucille's expression, Kid cracked.

"Yes," he murmured.

"You saw Clyde passing the *Hurdy* as you ran away, but it was a little distance off, I'm guessing. Not sure if he had seen you, and worried he would blab the fact innocently to his mother, you scrawled that ugly word on the door to frighten him. But Clyde's uncomplicated mind did not connect the hated word to what he had seen in the early hours of that morning."

Head hanging almost to his chest, Kid muttered, "He stopped by the club to bring something for Mizz Bassett 'round lunch time and asked me what I was doing up so late. It was then I knew."

"Y'all strangled my baby?" cried Eula Mae, Beau restraining her so that she wouldn't kill Kid right where he stood, in front of all these witnesses.

"It was him or my wife," Kid groaned.

"Care to explain?" Dodo demanded.

Covering his face with his hands he began, "G-gamblin'. I got in over my head with the gamblin'. I didn't mean it to happen, but an old pal 'a mine took me along to a more hardline group a' cardsters. I won big at first. Th…then it all changed and I was losin' every time. More broke than the Ten Commandments, I was. But I just knew if I could keep at it long enough, I'd come out on top. But it never happened. I got in deeper 'n deeper. Then the shark I owed threatened to hurt my wife and take my house." His yearning eyes seemed to plead with everyone in the room to understand his plight. "My wife, she's sick and it would kill her to know how I'd failed her and that we were gonna lose the house."

The bitter taste of aversion lingered on Dodo's tongue. "Someone heard about your predicament and offered you a way to erase your debt."

Head at an angle like it was too heavy to hold up, Kid continued his confession. "Auggie. He had it all planned out so no one would get hurt. And I *needed* the cash." His head sunk into his hands again. "It was dumb luck that I see'd Clyde as I was runnin' away. He looked in my d'rection but I was gone in a flash. I couldn't be sure he hadn't seen me, so instead of goin' to bed, I took me some old paint and gave him a warnin' to keep his mouth shut." His cheeks glistened. "I didn't wanna kill that chil', Mizz Eula Mae." He broke down in sobs.

Eula Mae struggled against Beau's grip and spit in Kid's face. "Clyde was all I had," she wailed.

"What about Mizz Dorchester's fiancé?" growled Lucille, not ready to let Kid go before he had confessed to everything.

"I just wanted her to stop investigatin'. My gals have 'em some rough husbands. I got 'em to help. Told 'em this guy was givin' me trouble, that I needed to send 'im a message he couldn't misunderstand. But I didn't tell 'em to hit him. I'm right sorry 'bout that ma'am."

He wiped the tears away like they were burning his skin. "I told Auggie the problem and he agreed to let me stash Mr. Danforth at *Lafitte's* for a few hours, 'til I decided what to do with him."

So, Auggie had lied. He *did* know who set the explosions. She found she wasn't that surprised.

Kid sniffed hard. "Then I remembered I used to play in that cave at the docks as a boy." Kid's brow knitted. "I was gonna send you a note where to find him after twenty-four hours. I swear. You just got to him sooner."

Rigatti stood. "I'll make sure Lieutenant Badger arrests this lowlife scumbag, Lulu." He gave a two-finger salute and stole out of the club.

Chapter 23

Both Eula Mae and Lucille were numb with shock.

How could the killer be Kid, the man they both loved like a cousin and had known most of their lives? It was like they had suffered a third tragedy.

Reluctantly, Badger had come to arrest Kid. He handcuffed and jerked him away to sit in a jail cell awaiting trial while they all looked on.

Though the ladies were still dazed, Dodo still had a couple of unanswered questions.

"Eula Mae, a flat package was delivered to your house the day of the tragedy. Did you ever see it?"

"I didn't, but I think maybe Clyde did. I found warm ashes in the fireplace the night he died, and I know I cleaned out the grate back in February. No one in their right mind would make a fire in this swelterin' heat. I moved the ashes around with a poker and saw the corner of a photograph. Clyde tried to destroy them."

"Do you think they were compromising snapshots?" Dodo asked.

If Eula Mae hadn't been emotionally drained dry, her cheeks would have flushed. "I think maybe so. I started seeing someone a few weeks ago."

"Why would anyone want to remove them from your house before you saw them if the pictures were just of you?" asked Dodo.

A light went on in Eula Mae's dreary eyes, "That no good son of a gun! I bet he was cheating on me!"

Rupert had encouraged Dodo to make the promised visit to Mrs. Dolby, Dex's mother, even though he was still in too much pain to go with her.

Where Dex was tall, his mother was petite—her feet hung two inches short of the ground as she sat in her plush armchair in the airy, comfortable home her son had purchased for her.

Mrs. Dolby ran a self-conscious hand over hair white as coconut meat. Smiling through brand new teeth, she welcomed Dodo like a long-lost friend.

"Mizz Dorchester! I'm happy as a pig in wallow to meet y'all. Come here and sit by me." She held out a hand that had seen more than its fair share of work. Grabbing Dodo's hand, she held it on her lap.

"What with all that bizzness, I didn't think you'd have time to visit an old lady," she admitted her voice almost worn out. "But my Dex said you were the kind of woman who keeps your word."

Dodo flashed Dex a smile. "That was sweet of him."

"Now, tell me all about the palace you live in. Do you have tea with the queen often?"

It had been four months since Lonnie Chapman, former pianist for *Smokey Syncopation*, and longtime personal friend of Lucille Bassett, had been murdered in London. Out of necessity, his actual funeral had taken place in England, so this memorial was all about celebrating his life.

Dodo wondered at the lively parade, led by the newly engaged Lucille. Could the Mardi Gras parades themselves rival this one? The whole town was decked out in the brightest colors the fabric stores could provide. Vivid bunting stretched all the way down Bourbon and Canal Streets.

The jazz band community was tight-knit, and Lucille had invited every band from uptown and downtown to participate. Jubilant, spirited music filled the streets and folks dressed in crazy carnival wear followed behind the line, waving feathers and flags. Dodo couldn't help but smile.

Lucille had promised to bring the parade past her house so that Rupert, who was still recuperating from his beating, could witness the splendor, but Beau had gone one better. He had hired a horse drawn carriage and settled Dodo and Rupert with Ernie and Lizzie right in the middle of the parade. Dodo waved until her arms ached.

Children lined the streets of the crescent-shaped city, joining the end of the parade with dancing and hollering. Dodo spotted Buddy and his family.

Every store and office opened their doors wide to pay their respects to a man who was a legend. Men and women hooted and cheered as the parade passed by under the blazing sun. It seemed the whole city was partying in honor of a good man who had been killed before his time.

Lonnie would have loved the party.

Dodo stared at her temporary engagement ring. She was finally going to be Mrs. Rupert Danforth. They had sent a telegram to both their parents and received congratulations in return.

Rupert was still black and blue, his ribs stabbing with every breath, but she didn't care. He was hers and that was all that mattered. In sickness and in health. She was happy to be his nurse.

"What?" he asked, catching her watching him.

"In spite of all the tragedy around us, I've never been so happy," she declared.

Raising the delicate mask that covered Dodo's eyes, Rupert laid a whisper of a kiss on her lips.

The crowd went wild.

The End

157

Thanks for buying my book!

Ann Sutton

I hope you enjoyed book 11, *Murder in New Orleans* and love Dodo as much as I do.

Interested in a **free** prequel to the Dodo Dorchester Mystery series?

Go to https://dl.bookfunnel.com/997vvive24 to download *Mystery at the Derby*.

Book *1* of the series, *Murder at Farrington Hall* is available on Amazon.

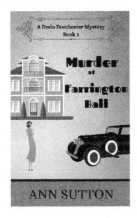

https://amzn.to/31WujyS

"Dodo is invited to a weekend party at Farrington Hall. She and her sister are plunged into sleuthing when a murder occurs. Can she solve the crime before Scotland Yard's finest?"

Book *2* of the series, *Murder is Fashionable* is available on Amazon.

https://amzn.to/2HBshwT

"Stylish Dodo Dorchester is a well-known patron of fashion. Hired by the famous Renee Dubois to support her line of French designs, she travels between Paris and London frequently. Arriving for the showing of the Spring 1923 collection, Dodo is thrust into her role as an amateur detective when one of the fashion models is murdered. Working under the radar of the French DCJP Inspector Roget, she follows clues to solve the crime. Will the murderer prove to be the man she has fallen for?"

Book *3* of the series, *Murder at the Races* is available on Amazon.

"It is royal race day at Ascot, 1923. Lady Dorothea Dorchester, Dodo, has been invited by her childhood friend, Charlie, to an exclusive party in a private box with the added incentive of meeting the King and Queen. Charlie appears to be interested in something more than friendship when a murder interferes with his plans. The victim is one of the guests from the box and Dodo cannot resist poking around. When Chief Inspector Blood of Scotland Yard is assigned to the case, sparks fly between them again. The chief inspector and Dodo have worked together on a case before and he welcomes her assistance with the prickly upper-class suspects. But where does this leave poor Charlie?
Dodo eagerly works on solving the murder which may have its roots in the distant past. Can she find the killer before they strike again?"

Book 4 of the series, *Murder on the Moors* is available on Amazon.

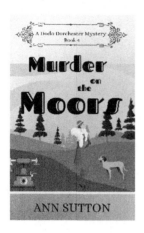

https://amzn.to/38SDX8d

When you just want to run away and nurse your broken heart but murder comes knocking.

"Lady Dorothea Dorchester, Dodo, flees to her cousins' estate in Dartmoor in search of peace and relaxation after her devastating break-up with Charlie and the awkward attraction to Chief Inspector Blood that caused it. Horrified to learn that the arch-nemesis from her schooldays, Veronica Shufflebottom, has been invited, Dodo prepares for disappointment. However, all that pales when one of the guests disappears after a ramble on the foggy moors. Presumed dead, Dodo attempts to contact the local police to report the disappearance only to find that someone has tampered with the ancient phone. The infamous moor fog is too thick for safe travel and the guests are therefore stranded.
Can Dodo solve the case without the help of the police before the fog lifts?"

Book 5 of the series, *Murder in Limehouse* is available on Amazon.

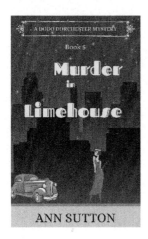

Aristocratic star she may be, but when her new love's sister is implicated in a murder, Dodo Dorchester rolls up her designer sleeves and plunges into the slums of London.

Dodo is back from the moors of Devon and diving into fashion business for the House of Dubois with one of the most celebrated department stores in England, while she waits for a call from Rupert Danforth, her newest love interest.

Curiously, the buyer she met with at the store, is murdered that night in the slums of Limehouse. It is only of passing interest because Dodo has no real connection to the crime. Besides, pursuing the promising relationship that began in Devon is a much higher priority.

However, fate has a different plan. Rupert's sister, Beatrice, is arrested for the murder of the very woman Dodo conducted business with at the fashionable store. Now she must solve the crime to protect the man she is fast falling in love with.

Can she do it before Beatrice is sent to trial?

Book 6 of the series, *Murder on Christmas Eve,* is available on Amazon.

Dodo is invited to meet Rupert's family for Christmas. What could possibly go wrong?

Fresh off the trauma of her last case, Dodo is relieved when Rupert suggests spending Christmas with his family at Knightsbrooke Priory.
The week begins with such promise until Rupert's grandmother, Adelaide, dies in the middle of their Christmas Eve dinner. She is ninety-five years old and the whole family considers it an untimely natural death, but something seems off to Dodo who uses the moment of shock to take a quick inventory of the body. Certain clues bring her to draw the conclusion that Adelaide has been murdered, but this news is not taken well.
With multiple family skeletons set rattling in the closets, the festive week of celebrations goes rapidly downhill and

Dodo fears that Rupert's family will not forgive her meddling. Can she solve the case and win back their approval?

Book *7* of the series, *Murder on the Med* is available on Amazon.

https://amzn.to/3P0oO99

An idyllic Greek holiday. A murdered ex-pat. Connect the victim to your tourist party, and you have a problem that only Dodo can solve.

Dodo's beau, Rupert, is to meet the Dorchesters for the first time on their annual Greek holiday. He arrives in Athens by train and her family accept him immediately. But rather than be able to enjoy private family time, an eclectic group of English tourists attach themselves to the Dorchesters, and insist on touring the Parthenon with them.

Later that night, a body is found in the very area they had visited and when Dodo realizes that it is the woman she saw earlier, near the hotel, staring at someone in their group, she cannot help but get involved. The over-worked and under-staffed local detective is more than happy for her assistance and between them they unveil all the tourists' dirty secrets.

With help from Rupert and Dodo, can the detective discover the murderer and earn himself a promotion?

Book 8 of the series, *Murder Spoils the Fair* is available on Amazon

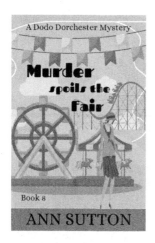

https://amzn.to/42xldFn

A high profile national fair, a murdered model. Can Dodo solve the crime before it closes the fair?

The historic British Empire Fair of 1924 is set to be officially opened by the king at the new Wembley Stadium and Lady Dorothea Dorchester, Dodo, has an invitation.

The whole fair is an attempt to build morale after a devastating World War and the planning and preparation have been in the works for years. So much is riding on its success.

The biggest soap maker in England has been offered the opportunity to host a beauty exhibit and after a nationwide search for the ten most beautiful girls in Britain, they build an extravagant 'palace' that will feature live models representing famous women of history, including one who will represent today's modern woman. Dodo has succeeded in winning the bid to clothe Miss 1924 with fashions from the House of Dubois for whom she is a fashion ambassador.

But the fair has hardly begun when disaster strikes. One of the models is murdered. Can Dodo find the murderer before the bad PR closes the fair?

Book *9* of the series, *Murder Takes a Swing* is available on Amazon.

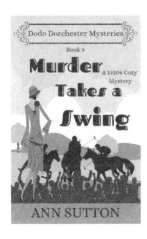

https://amzn.to/3sg3Wn0

High stakes, dark secrets, murder and mayhem. Can Dodo find the killer of Rupert's polo teammate without endangering their love in the process?

In Murder Takes A Swing, Dodo Dorchester finds herself drawn deep into the glamorous world of polo when one of her beaus' teammates is found murdered the night after their victorious first game of the season.

With the sport of kings as its backdrop, this gripping and unputdownable page-turner will keep you on the edge of your seat as Rupert's friends and teammates become the prime suspects in this deadly game of hidden secrets.

Dodo must use her wits to untangle a web of deceit and betrayal that threatens to unravel everything Rupert thought he knew about his friends. Will she be able to solve the case before the killer strikes again? Can their developing relationship endure the strain?

Full of charm, and suspense, this delightful 1920s cozy mystery will transport you back in time to a world of adventure, and danger, keeping you on the edge of your seat until the very last twist.

Perfect for fans of classic murder mystery novels and historical whodunnits, this is a book you won't want to miss. So, grab your mallet and join the game – the stakes are high and the secrets are deadly.

Book 10 of the series, *Murder Goes Jazz* is available on Amazon.

Solving a murder in the Big Easy is anything but.

After an invitation to visit New Orleans from Miss Lucille Bassett, famous jazz singer, Dodo and company board a luxury ocean liner and head across the pond. The climate, the food and the culture couldn't be more different from England and Dodo considers the whole trip a grand adventure.

Enjoying her role as tourist, Dodo delights in a trip on a steamer down the Mississippi, a visit to an ancient smuggler's dwelling and the hustle and bustle of Bourbon Street. At the top of her wish list, however, is dancing at Miss Bassett's famous jazz club.

On their second day in Louisiana, a terrible murder occurs without any obvious motive. Lucille implores Dodo to take the case as gangsters abound in the Prohibition Era South and have the police department in their pockets.

Dodo agrees but her sleuthing places a loved one in danger and she is torn between solving the crime for her friend or protecting those she loves.

Curl up with this delightful, pager-turner of a whodunnit that will have you on the edge of your seat until the last chapter.

I am also pleased to announce that I have created a new series, the Percy Pontefract Mysteries. Book 1, *Death at a Christmas Party: A 1920's Cozy Mystery,* is available now on Amazon.

https://amzn.to/3Qb4BhG

A merry Christmas party with old friends. A dead body in the kitchen. A reluctant heroine. Sounds like a recipe for a jolly festive murder mystery!

"It is 1928 and a group of old friends gather for their annual Christmas party. The food, drink and goodwill flow, and everyone has a rollicking good time.

When the call of nature forces the accident-prone Percy Pontefract up, in the middle of the night, she realizes she is in need of a little midnight snack and wanders into the kitchen. But she gets more than she bargained for when she trips over a dead body.

Ordered to remain in the house by the grumpy inspector sent to investigate the case, Percy stumbles upon facts about her friends that shake her to the core and cause her to suspect more than one of them of the dastardly deed.

Finally permitted to go home, Percy tells her trusty cook all the awful details. Rather than sympathize, the cook encourages her to do some investigating of her own. After all, who knows these people better than Percy? Reluctant at first, Percy begins poking into her friends' lives, discovering they all harbor dark secrets. However, none seem connected to the murder...at first glance.

Will Percy put herself and her children in danger before she can solve the case that has the police stumped?"

Book 2 of the Percy Pontefract Mysteries, *Death is a Blank Canvasy: A 1920's Cozy Mystery,* is also available on Amazon.

https://amzn.to/3P6SrY7

An invitation-only art exhibition. A rising star cut down in his prime. The only suspects, family and a handful of aristocrats. How will Percy navigate these treacherous waters to solve the callous crime?

In this gripping sequel, Percy Pontefract finds herself entangled in a twisted web of murder and lies that strikes painfully close to home, when her talented cousin is brutally killed as the curtain rises on his inaugural modern art exhibition in the heart of London.

The shadow of suspicion looms over everyone present; Percy's colorful relatives and a number of enigmatic aristocrats. When circumstances thrust Percy into detection, she is soon caught up in a dangerous game of cat and mouse as she unravels the truth and concludes that the solution to the murder lies beneath layers of paint, privilege and pretension. She must rely on intuition and luck to avoid becoming the next victim.

Set against a backdrop of the glamorous world of fine art and filled with a cast of eccentric characters, Death Is a Blank Canvas, is a rollicking good whodunnit that will keep you guessing until the very end.

For more information about both series go to my website at www.annsuttonauthor.com and subscribe to my newsletter.

You can also follow me on Facebook at:
https://www.facebook.com/annsuttonauthor

About the Author

Agatha Christie plunged me into the fabulous world of reading when I was 10. I was never the same. I read every one of her books I could lay my hands on. Mysteries remain my favorite genre to this day - so it was only natural that I would eventually write my own.

Born and raised in England, writing fiction about my homeland keeps me connected.

After finishing my degree in French and Education and raising my family, writing has become a favorite hobby.

I hope that Dame Agatha would enjoy Dodo Dorchester at much as I do.

Acknowledgements

I would like to thank all those who read my books, write reviews and provide suggestions as you continue to inspire.

My proof-reader – Tami Stewart

The mother of a large and growing family who reads like the wind with an eagle eye. Thank you for finding little errors that have been missed.

My editors at Waypoint Authors.

They provide insightful suggestions while not crushing my tender ego.

My cheerleader, marketer and IT guy – Todd Matern

A lot of the time during the marketing side of being an author I am running around with my hair on fire. Todd is the yin to my yang. He calms me down and takes over when I am yelling at the computer.

My beta readers – Francesca Matern, Stina Van Cott

Your reactions to my characters and plot are invaluable.

The Writing Gals for their FB author community and their YouTube tutorials

These ladies give so much of their time to teaching their Indie author followers how to succeed in this brave new publishing world. Thank you.

20BooksTo50K for their support of all indie authors and their invaluable knowledge of the indie publishing world.

Printed in Great Britain
by Amazon

36095002R00106